THE LIES WE LOVED

BELLE S OWENS

ISBN: 978-1-7642099-1-5

To Finley, your courage gave me courage.

DISCLAIMER

Please note that although this book is set in New York City, I am an Australian author therefore some spelling and words will reflect that.

CONTENT WARNING

This novel contains themes that some readers may find distressing, including references to suicide and suicidal ideation, pregnancy complications and child illness. Reader discretion is advised.

CHAPTER ONE

People always come into your life for a reason, a season or a
lifetime. Embrace each for what they are meant to be
- Brian A. "Drew" Chalker

Paige

P aige had lived by this philosophy her whole life. It had
rattled around in her brain when her high school sweetheart broke her heart right before graduation. It had helped her as she
mourned the loss of her best friend before her 21st birthday. It had
been there as she helped pick up the pieces of her mother's heart after
her father ran off with their next door neighbour. All these significant
moments in her life had made her the woman she was now - the fear-

less, strong, logical and independent woman who stood in the pouring rain on an uncharacteristically cold night in October, as the man she had devoted herself to for three years confessed his feelings for another woman.

Heather. The name rolled off his tongue, and Paige's world tilted on its axis. An executive producer on his latest project. She had known they'd grown closer in recent months but, hearing the name spoken aloud, heavy with meaning, blindsided her. She stood frozen, an unwilling audience to his monologue.

His eyes lit up as he spun his confession, weaving a web of deceit, blind to the way her heart splintered into a million pieces at his feet. He spoke of Heather as if his words were poetry, their friendship blooming into something more, something inevitable. He couldn't remember when it began, only that it had consumed him. And now, he said, he could no longer hold it back; he could no longer let Paige stand in the way of the love story he believed was his.

A thousand thoughts ran through her head, but the most poignant one was when did he stop thinking of her like this? She could tell how much he cared about Heather. She saw it in the dreamy smile that spread slowly across his face like sunlight breaking through a morning mist as he recalled a stolen moment. She heard it in the soft gentle laugh that escaped his lips like a feather landing on still water, barely making a ripple. She felt it as his nervous excitement cut the distance between them, creating an ever-growing chasm that smashed the fragile scaffolding of the world they had created.

She couldn't recall the moment things changed; the exact point in time where he fell out of love. She was blindsided by his confession and embarrassed at not having seen his betrayal coming.

For a fleeting moment, Paige was transported back to the first day she met Elliot. He'd stood in the entry of the old coffee shop, rain plastered to his chocolate brown curls, green eyes shining with reckless hope. She'd been nervous, worrying she'd make a fool of herself in front of the rising star playing the lead in her debut novel's film.

Elliot crossed the room in quick strides, towering over her with that easy, wide smile. As he offered to take her dripping coat she realised the anxiety had dulled her senses to the winter rain. One kind gesture had led to other meetings about scripts, and soon the excuses fell away. The meetings were just about them. What started out as a professional friendship soon turned into a budding relationship. During the last three years they had become completely in-sync... or so she thought. Dinners with her family celebrating milestones, Sunday mornings at the Farmers Market, relaxing on the lounge watching their show, inside jokes - when they were together the mundane became extraordinary.

Standing in the rain now, Paige hugged her arms around herself, shivering not from the cold, but from the razor sharp words Elliot had just thrown at her. He wasn't just closing the door on their relationship; he was nailing it shut, sealing every crack, leaving no sliver of hope.

"Why are you telling me now?" Paige asked, her voice struggling to be heard over the sound of the icy rain that was slowly drowning her.

"I'm sorry, P," Elliot whispered, his voice faltering as he took a tentative step towards her. "I know there's no easy way to say this... but I can't keep living this lie. I've been lying to you, to myself... and it's killing me. I can't pretend anymore - not with you, not with her. I never meant for any of this to happen but, somewhere along the way, things changed. I don't want to hurt you; God knows I don't, but I've fallen in love with Heather and I can't keep dragging you along like this."

He took a shaky breath, his eyes searching hers for forgiveness, for acceptance; anything to rid him of the guilt that had settled in his stomach and solidified like rock. It was a constant reminder of his infidelity but there was no answer. There was no comfort in her expression, only her stark pain that cut through his words.

"I'm sorry, God, I'm so sorry for doing this here, in the middle of the street, with the whole world watching. I should've taken you somewhere quiet, somewhere we could talk; where I could at least give you the decency of a proper conversation. Not... this. Not like this."

He ran a hand through his hair, the words tumbling out faster than he could catch them. "I wish I could take it all back. Every lie, every excuse. But I can't. I've made my choice and… it's her."

His voice cracked, but he didn't stop. "The truth is, you deserve more than this. More than me. You deserve someone who loves you the way you need to be loved, not someone who can't even decide if you're enough."

He took a breath, but it didn't steady him. "I can't be that person for you anymore." A concealed betrayal masked by dazzling green eyes.

Paige felt her heart sink and her pulse began to roar in her ears. His voice was muffled, almost as if it came from underwater. The words hit her like cold water, soaking through her skin and into her soul, leaving her numb and hollow. It took a beat - just one - before the weight of it all sank in. It was suffocating. Her chest tightened, her breath caught, and her legs felt like stone. It wasn't just his words, but the finality of them. There was no taking them back. There was no going back.

This had not been part of her plans for the evening. She had thought tonight would be the night the love of her life asked her the one simple question she'd been waiting a long time to hear. Paige had thought his choice in restaurant had had a hidden meaning. It was their favourite, yes, but it was also the location of their first official date. Now, barely two blocks away, it was a mocking presence. Elliot's confession had carved a canyon between them.

The lights of Manhattan flickered above them, casting shadows across Elliot's face. Paige tried to focus on his features, the ones she had memorised so carefully over the years. His jaw was tight, his eyes wide with guilt. Where was the man she once knew? The man she had loved? As she looked at him, the veil lifted. This wasn't the man who had shared her hopes and dreams, who had promised her forever. No, this man standing before her was a stranger, and her heart sank beneath the weight of that realisation. She wanted to scream, to ask him how he could do this to her, but instead she just stood there. The man she had known was gone, replaced by a stranger she didn't recognise.

Paige shook her head, trying to wake from this nightmare. She wiped her eyes, erasing all emotion from her expression. She would no longer give him the satisfaction of seeing the pain he had inflicted. Without a word, Paige turned and walked away, her steps slow and deliberate as her mind raced. As if in a dream, she moved towards their apartment, her heart heavy with confusion and disbelief. Their home was theirs no longer. It was now hers. Cars sped by, but the only thing that mattered was putting distance between herself and the man who had shattered her world.

Stepping over the threshold, Paige made a beeline for the bathroom where she caught sight of her reflection. Her usually wavy chestnut hair clung to her face - drenched, limp and lifeless. Her amber eyes were glassy with further unshed tears, red and swollen; drained of emotion, unable to convey the depth of her sorrow. She recalled the effort she had put into her appearance a few short hours ago. The time spent curling each section of hair, the crisp lines of eyeliner she had fretted over getting perfect. The hard work now undone.

Her gaze flicked to the bin in the corner and, once again, her heart stalled mid-beat. Bending down, she reached for the object that had caught her eye. The white stick, so innocuous at first glance, still showed the two pink lines from this morning - lines that had filled her with disbelief, a flicker of anxiety and then a steady, rising anticipation she could barely find within herself now. The reality of the future she had planned was now gone. The excitement that once pressed warm against her ribs had now thinned into something colder, quieter, leaving her staring at the proof of a life that no longer fitted the shape of her own.

What was she supposed to do now?

CHAPTER TWO

The first light slipped through the cracks in the shutters, catching on the quiet wreckage of the night before and pulling her back to herself. Paige felt her stiff muscles protest as she rose off the cold hard tiles where she had remained all night. For hours she had stared at the floor, studying the grey, monochromatic tiles, suddenly aware that their random placement reflected the chaos within her mind. Her eyes honed in on a cracked tile, half hidden by the basket that housed her washing. It was not overtly noticeable, but it was there. Enough to threaten the structural integrity of the floor if left untreated. Was that a metaphor for her relationship? Had there been cracks but her attention was focused elsewhere so she didn't see the undercurrent fractures threatening the stability of her relationship?

Rising up she locked eyes with the stranger in the mirror. Heavy bags now joined what was left of her makeup streaming down her cheeks and her hair had dried into a halo of frizz. She was the antithesis of the person she was when she left the apartment the night before. Her reflection was cruel. Mocking.

She moved towards the shower and turned the tap to full blast in an effort to wash away the painful memories of yesterday. The water scalded her skin as she stepped into it and she welcomed its embrace, the pain nothing compared to what she had experienced last night. Elliot's words had settled like lead in her stomach, leaking poison through her body. With all her might, Paige tried to lift her arms to wash herself but even that felt too hard. Internally she screamed at her arms to move, to lift the shampoo and run her fingers through her hair but they refused. Instead she stood beneath the torrent of water while her mind ran wild. Once upon a time, Elliot would have joined her in the shower. She would have savoured the feeling of his fingers dragging across her scalp as he softly massaged in the shampoo. Each movement would have sent her mind floating, a sense of calm washing over her and her body collapsing into a sea of serenity. Trapped in a spiral of fixation, her gaze drifted around the shower, taking in the small, ordinary pieces of their life together - pieces that suddenly felt like artefacts from a lost world.

The bamboo toothbrush she'd bought him, part of her gentle campaign to make him more eco friendly, stuck to the wall. He had laughed when she gave it to him, but kissed her and thanked her anyway. His joy was so sincere at the time, it made her heart swell. Now, that memory cut her open.

Stepping out, Paige moved to grab the closest towel but stopped at the sight of his embroidered initials, which marked it as his. Would she want to keep her matching towel if his made its home somewhere else? Surely he'd be taking these items to Heather's place. The thought pushed Paige further into the dark, swallowing her whole.

He was in love with someone else.

When did it happen? Paige couldn't pinpoint it exactly. Sure, every day he'd come home from set raving about Heather. Her brilliance, her insights, her wealth of knowledge - it was like he was in awe of her. On his days off, his phone would often ring, her name lighting up the screen. Whenever Paige asked what they were talking about, he'd brushed it off. Just work stuff, he'd say. Maybe it was. Maybe it wasn't. Either way, that should have been her first clue.

She had trusted him. Blindly. The sun rose and set with him, and for a long time, she was happy to orbit around his world. The thought made bile rise in her throat, bitter and sharp. She scoffed at her own naivety. Maybe it had been a one-sided love story all along. Somewhere along the way, she had stopped being his equal and had become a supporting character in his life. She had stopped voicing opinions about the scripts he brought home; stopped asking him to watch her favourite movies because they weren't his thing. When had her edges softened to fit neatly into the spaces he allowed?

Her eyes drifted to her stomach, which she now noticed was slightly rounded. She had suspected for weeks now that she might be pregnant. They were intimate almost every chance they got and contraception wasn't something they had paid much mind to. Looking back, the signs were there. The missed periods she had blamed on stress, the fatigue she had chalked up to long nights and looming deadlines. With her final book nearing release, life had been a blur of meetings, edits and reviews. As the closing chapter to her bestselling series, the pressure to meet her own demanding standards and the expectations of her publisher and agent was relentless.

Three missed periods.

That put her around the twelve week mark. She hadn't seen a doctor yet, hadn't even said the words out loud. But yesterday's test was all the confirmation she needed.

Paige had planned to tell Elliot last night. She'd even practised the words in her head, rehearsed them in front of the mirror until they felt almost real. But the moment he walked through the door, she knew something was off. His words were warm enough, but his smile never reached his eyes. There was a distance between them, subtle but undeniable. Like he was wearing a mask, something polite and paper thin, just to get through the evening.

Now, she understood why.

Was he being intimate with Heather while he was with her?

The thought crossed Paige's mind, and it felt like being hit by a truck all over again. Sudden, brutal, leaving her breathless. But this time, no tears came. She was empty.

Her head dropped, hands instinctively smoothing the small swell of her stomach. She traced slow circles, trying to soothe the ache in her chest. What now? Every option felt like a landmine waiting to detonate. If she told Elliot, there were three ways this could go. He might choose her, choose their family and somehow they'd piece themselves back together. Or he might stay with Heather, promising to co-parent and 'be there' in whatever empty way men like him always claimed. Or worst of all, he might walk away entirely, leaving Paige and the baby to navigate the fallout alone.

Every path hurt. There was no version of this that didn't leave her bleeding.

The idea of him choosing her - choosing them - was good in theory. But he had already planted the seed of doubt now and she was unsure if she could overlook it. If he could choose Heather once, what would stop him from choosing her, or someone else, again? Paige knew herself well enough to know that she couldn't live her life wondering if every late night, every unanswered text, was the start of another betrayal. The idea of raising a child in a home built on that kind of uncertainty made her stomach churn.

Co-parenting, on paper, seemed like the sensible middle ground. In reality, she knew it would be anything but simple. Could she really stay tethered to him while he wrapped his life around someone new? The idea of having to share her child with a stranger and with the man who betrayed her was hard to envisage.

If she were being truly honest, the third scenario didn't terrify her as much as it probably should. The baby would be hers - her responsibility, her constant - without opinions she didn't trust and without reminders of the night everything fell apart. She wouldn't have to relive their worst moments over and over.

The many thoughts ricocheted inside her skull, barbed and cruel. And worst of all, with so little information about how this affair even started, Paige couldn't be sure who was really at fault. Had Heather chased him? Set her sights on him from the start? Or had Elliot been the one to cross the line first, knowing exactly what was at stake? Paige shook her head sharply, as if that could physically dislodge the spiralling questions from her brain. They clung like a disease, infecting every rational thought.

Raising a child in the rubble of Elliot's betrayal - with the doubt, the broken trust - meant building a home on a ground that wasn't stable. Paige feared what that would teach their child about love - that it could splinter or disappear. The future of three lives now lay with her.

Her head snapped toward the sound of her phone vibrating, the sharp ping shattering the silence. With trembling fingers, she fished it from the pocket of her jacket. The name on the screen sent a bolt of pain straight through her chest. Elliot.

> P, I'm sorry to bother you. I need to pick up some of my things. If you're not up for seeing me, I understand. I can ask Shaun or Toby to do it for me.

HER HEART JUMPED at the prospect of seeing him again, as if, despite the pain, her body still craved him like a lovesick puppy. Paige questioned his motives and her own. Was he simply here to collect his things, or was he wanting to survey the wreckage caused by his confession? The idea of the latter made her skin tingle with dread. This might be her chance for answers.

She tapped out her reply, granting permission for him to stop by, then dragged herself into action. A clean outfit revived her more than any cup of coffee could. Settling at the kitchen bench, pen in hand, she jotted down questions that felt both necessary and terrifying.

When did the affair start? Why did he cheat? How did it begin?

Her fingers hovered above the page, hesitating. Did she really want the answers?

A SOFT KNOCK echoed through the room. Paige stood, adjusting her shirt to hide the bulge she was certain he must have noticed over the past few weeks. When she opened the door, there he stood, the dark haired man she once saw as her missing puzzle piece.

He was a stranger now.

He looked the same, smelt the same, but something about him had shifted. She couldn't quite place it, but the man she had loved was no longer standing in front of her. Or maybe, she realised, she was the one who had changed overnight.

His smile was small, polite, the kind you give to someone at the supermarket, not the woman you once professed you couldn't live without.

"Thanks for letting me come by," he murmured, shifting uneasily on his feet. His discomfort was obvious, and normally it would trigger her instinct to smooth things over, to comfort him. But now, she just couldn't. She wouldn't.

Instead, a wave of fury rushed through her, hot and searing. How dare he turn up at her home and have the audacity to look uncomfortable. This was his fault. Her sorrow and devastation had faded, replaced by a red hot ball of rage that burned deep inside her, spreading like wildfire, threatening to consume everything in its wake.

In that moment, she wanted to punch him. To strike that perfect face.

She had never felt this way before. Sure, there had been boyfriends who had cheated on her in her past, but nothing had hurt like this. She had pledged herself to him completely, and this... this was a betrayal of a different calibre.

"Before you get your stuff, I have questions and I think I'm entitled to answers." Paige was almost startled by her own voice. It was calm, detached, a stark contrast to the heat burning in her chest.

"Yeah... of course. I owe you that."

The last thing Elliot wanted was to hurt the woman he had once loved, but the way Paige barely seemed to care wasn't what he expected. Had none of it meant anything to her? Had *he* meant nothing?

His gaze followed her through the apartment they had once shared. Everything about her was familiar, yet foreign. Fragments of their life together lay scattered across the pristine space, and a faint smile tugged at his lips. Everything appeared as it always had, clean and organised. That was Paige. A planner to her core. Lists, schedules, colour-coded calendars. And yet, she was always the first to throw caution to the wind if adventure called. That perfect, beautiful contradiction.

He sank onto the lounge, inhaling the sweetness of home, a scent now painfully bittersweet. When his eyes found Paige again, her stoic expression set him further on edge. This wasn't the woman he remembered but, then again, maybe neither of them were the same people they were three years ago.

Elliot let out a soft chuckle as Paige pulled out a crumpled list from her pocket, the paper trembling slightly between her fingers.

"Ask whatever you need."

His voice was quiet, resigned to the fact that this would hurt. He knew the questions before she even asked. What he didn't know was if he had the answers she deserved.

Paige inhaled sharply.

"When did the affair start?"

Her voice was a flatline, stripped of feeling. It hurt like hell to keep it that way, but survival mode had kicked in. This wasn't just about heartbreak anymore; she was a mother now, and protecting her baby meant keeping herself together.

"I don't know," Elliot's voice wavered. "We've been working on this movie for months…"

"That's not what I asked." Paige's voice cut through the room like a blade. She could already hear the excuses forming, well rehearsed, carefully framed; and she wanted none of it. Facts. Just the fucking facts.

"Right. Yeah. Sorry." He dragged a hand through his hair, buying time. "It's just I don't know when it started."

"How could you not know?" The crack in her voice bled hostility, raw and unfamiliar even to herself. Elliot flinched. In all their years together, she'd never spoken to him like this, never sounded so hollow.

"It just happened," he mumbled.

"What happened, Elliot?" Her voice rose, clipped and shaking. "Did you sleep with her? Did you sneak off to see her? Sext her behind my back? Hell, did you do all three while I was at home, loving you like an idiot?" The dam burst, rage spilling out in waves. Her hands shook, her chest heaved, but she didn't care. Let him see. Let him feel it.

"I never did anything behind your back! I promise you! She doesn't even know I have feelings for her."

"She doesn't know? So you're leaving me for someone who doesn't even know you have feelings for her? You're throwing away three years - our home, our future - for a fantasy? Are you stupid?"

Paige barely recognised her own voice. Cutting, biting, unapologetic; she wanted him to feel every ounce of her pain, wanted her words to cut him open like he'd done to her. The venom shocked her, but she couldn't stop.

He ran a shaky hand through his hair, swallowing hard. He'd been drifting for months, caught somewhere between resentment and self loathing, losing his passion for acting while watching Paige thrive. She moved through the world with a certainty he'd never had - a solid path supported by a family who caught her every time she stumbled. He'd never had that. Not really. Of course he had his mum and he loved her fiercely. In the absence of his father she had carried both parent roles on her back and never once complained. It had always been the two of them, a world held together by her exhaustion and his determination not to make things harder. Over time he'd listened to the voices that said Paige didn't need him; the ones that said they weren't right for each other. Somewhere along the way, that envy curdled into something ugly. Something he couldn't explain, even to himself.

Elliot stood frozen, blindsided. Seeing her like this, all fire and fury, gutted him. He'd done this. He'd made her a stranger. And the worst part? She was right. This wasn't just about Paige. This was about him, falling out of love with himself.

When had he started competing with the woman he loved? Had he ever really wanted to win, or just not lose?

If he was being honest, he still loved Paige. More than he thought humanly possible. But Heather? Did he love her too? Or was he just grasping at something, anything, to fill the growing emptiness inside him? Last night, the guilt had eaten him alive. He'd confessed his feelings about Heather not because he was sure of them, but because he wasn't.

But now, replaying Paige's words in his head, he knew the truth. He'd messed up. Bad. His curiosity about Heather and his pathetic need for reassurance had blown up his entire life.

Paige crushed the paper in her fist and hurled it at his bowed head. How dare he! He had thrown their relationship away for something that might not even happen. What was she? A placeholder? Someone to warm his bed until someone better came along?

The thought made her stomach turn. A dark, ugly rage clawed its way to the surface, drowning out the last shreds of reason. Paige wasn't cruel; she never had been. But right now? She wanted him to hurt. Not just once. Not just now. A thousand cuts. Each one pointed enough to make him bleed.

"I hate you, Elliot. Get the hell out of my house." Her voice was low and deadly. Elliot's breath hitched as tears slipped down his face. The magnitude of it all sank in. He had lost her. For good. What had he done?

Paige mimicked his movements as he stood to leave. The air was thick with unspoken words, choking them both. He tried to stifle his sobs, but they broke through in ragged gasps. Not even a day ago, the sound of his pain would have shattered her. Today, it was music to her ears. She had given everything to this man, and it still wasn't enough.

He turned at the open door, as if searching for a final moment between them. Something flew towards him and he caught it instinctively. His breath caught as he looked down at a positive pregnancy test.

Before he could speak, Paige twisted the knife. "I never want to see you again. Stay the hell away from us." She slammed the door in his face. The rage drained from her body, leaving only the echo of her own words.

What had she done?

CHAPTER THREE

Dear little love,

Your father has left us.

Reading those words on this page doesn't feel real. I've repeated them to myself countless times, but they still feel like they belong in someone else's story. Not mine. Not ours.

I'm so hurt right now; overwhelmed in ways I can barely understand. I don't know what to think. How can I focus on the future when the memories of our past cut so deeply? The man I trusted most, the person I loved with every part of my being, became the very person who broke me in ways I never saw coming.

I hardly recognise the woman I am now - filled with anger, bitterness, sadness. My hopes, my dreams, have been shattered. And with that heartbreak, there is fear. A heavy, suffocating fear about what lies ahead.

I'm scared of doing this alone - scared of not being enough, of carrying the weight of every responsibility, every decision, every moment that lies ahead. It feels like too much for one heart to hold.

But my precious baby, there is one thing I need you to know with absolute certainty: None of this is your fault.

You are blameless. Innocent. Caught in the storm of someone else's choices.

I don't have all the answers yet, and I don't know if I ever will. But I can promise you this: this pain will not shape our lives. I will rebuild our world with whatever strength I can find.

I am scared, yes. But I am also determined.

For you.

Love,

Mumma

*P*aige let the pen slip from her fingers, pressing her head into her hands. What had she done? She had been asking herself that same question for days now.

To his credit, Elliot had listened; he had done exactly what she asked and stayed away. Instead of the relief she expected, all she felt was a deep visceral anger. Why didn't he fight for her? Did the baby mean nothing to him?

In the days since, Paige had booked her first doctor's appointment. Now, she sat in the waiting room, her heart hammering against her ribs while a stack of pamphlets lay scattered across her lap, filled with information that made her heart and her brain ache. *Vitamin K and Your Baby. The Positives of Breastfeeding. Your Birth Plan and You. Leaping into Fatherhood.* The last one felt like a slap to the face. Its big, bold letters staring back at her, taunting her.

A tear threatened to escape, but she forced a deep breath and lifted her head. The waiting room felt stifling, despite its size. It was filled with happy couples, drawn into their own conversations, oblivious to her loneliness.

In the corner, a little girl sat fiddling with a yellow Lego piece, her parents watching her every move intently. As she mumbled to herself, they exchanged a look of pride, of love. The kind of expression that screamed, 'We made this.' Paige felt their wonderment radiate from across the aisle. And with it came the familiar ache, the one that had taken up residence in her chest since that fateful night.

"Ms. Lawson?"

The voice pulled Paige back from her spiralling thoughts. She looked up, offering a weak smile as she stood. A plump woman with a warm expression waited expectantly for her, radiating a kindness that took her by surprise.

"I'm Jenny," the woman introduced herself, her Southern accent unmistakable.

Paige must have been exuding anxiety because, a moment later, a gentle hand rested on her arm, its warmth startling her slightly.

"It's okay, honey," Jenny said reassuringly. "That first appointment'll rattle anyone. Is this your first?"

She ushered Paige into the room, barely giving her a chance to answer before continuing.

"I was the same way with my first," Jenny said with a nostalgic smile. "I wasn't long outta school when I met my Roger and before I knew it, we were blessed with our firstborn. I remember feelin' like I was starin' into the face of the unknown. But you don't have a thing to worry about, honey. Just a few questions before Dr Baker comes in."

She glanced at Paige eagerly. "You didn't say before, is this your first baby?"

Paige nodded, gripping her handbag tighter against her chest. The hard plastic of the chair pressed uncomfortably against her back, grounding her in the moment.

"Is daddy coming along today?"

Though Jenny's tone was gentle, the words sliced through Paige like a red hot razor.

"Ah, no. No. He…umm…isn't in the picture," Paige said, her voice faltering as she averted her gaze.

A flicker of embarrassment crossed Jenny's face but, before she could say anything more, a brisk knock at the door cut through the tension. Without waiting for a response, the door swung open, revealing yet another unfamiliar face.

"Ms. Lawson, it's nice to meet you. I'm Liam Baker, and I'll be looking after you for the next few months."

His smile was friendly and, for a brief moment, the weight pressing down on her chest seemed to ease a fraction. As he moved to the machine beside her, Paige took in his appearance. Though his white lab coat provided few hints as to what lay underneath, she could just make out a crisp blue cotton shirt, the second button from the top undone revealing a hint of warm brown skin, perhaps more than necessary. He looked effortlessly put together, a blend of professionalism and ease.

And then, unexpectedly, she felt long forgotten stirrings - that warm, trembling ripple she remembered all too well from the first moment she met Elliot, back before everything broke.

"So, how about we meet this baby?" His smile spread across his face, revealing his perfect white teeth. Paige was momentarily overwhelmed by the weight of the simple question. Was she really ready to meet the baby? Her baby? Until now, the little life inside her had been nothing more than a thought - a possibility.

But now it was becoming real. Tangible. Life-changing.

Her throat tightened as the magnitude of this moment hit her. This would be *the* moment - the one she remembered forever. Unable to do anything but nod, she laid back and pulled up her shirt, trying to steady her racing heart.

Doctor Baker squeezed the cool gel onto her stomach and Paige stiffened, her body tensing with anticipation. For a moment, it felt as though the world stopped spinning as the transducer glided over her skin in slow, deliberate strokes. She couldn't bring herself to look at the screen. Fixing her gaze on the ceiling, she counted the multitude of small pinprick holes in the plaster - anything to anchor herself against the swell of nerves rising inside her.

"Congratulations, you're 15 weeks along." His deep baritone voice broke through her foggy brain, the words slow to process. Fifteen weeks? Almost halfway there. A wave of disbelief washed over her, followed by a sense of urgency. She turned towards the screen.

And then she saw it. The baby.

It was unmistakable - a tiny, wriggling form dancing across the screen. Paige watched, mesmerised, as the baby threw wild kicks and punches, each movement fierce enough to startle, yet somehow too small to be felt. Yet. Her heart fluttered and the cement wall she had meticulously built around her emotions since that night began to crack, piece by piece.

She wasn't just carrying a baby; she was carrying someone who needed her. A fierce, instinctive urge rose within her - protective, primal, undeniable - and suddenly all of her doubts, her fears, and even her anger faded into the background. This was real. Whatever came next, she would do everything in her power to protect her child.

A part of Paige was angry that Elliot wasn't there to see it. Another part, almost shamefully, was relieved - selfishly pleased that she didn't have to share this moment. This was hers. Hers alone. A little human was growing inside her, emerging from something so painful. Emotions swirled within her, conflicting and raw, yet deep down she knew that the longer she waited to tell people about her news, the heavier the secret would become.

Since her bump had started to show, Paige had noticed how quickly her clothes were stretching. The media interviews were approaching, and soon the world would know. Surprisingly, the thought didn't terrify her as much as she had expected. Instead, a quiet joy had begun to rise, the idea of finally sharing the news filling her with joy.

Motherhood had never been a dream Paige chased. She wasn't

opposed to it, but had never before felt the pressing need to bear a child. Yet now, all she could think about was the life growing inside her. Every change in her body, each new sensation, filled her with a strange emotion she couldn't quite define.

Each morning she would stand in front of the mirror, studying her naked body. She traced every curve and line, every subtle change from the day before, feeling a growing connection to the life she carried.

Even with this wonder, her emotions remained turbulent. One moment, she marvelled at her body's transformation, basking in the glow of her changing self. The next, grief crashed over her, holding her heart prisoner as she mourned the loss of her relationship.

Over the past few days, she had replayed every moment of their time together, dissecting every interaction, trying to pinpoint where things had gone wrong. Had she given too little, expected too much, loved in the wrong way? Each question dug deeper, and still, the answers eluded her.

The questions frothed relentlessly in her mind as she sat in the back of the cab, on her way to visit her mum and finally tell her the news. With things unfolding the way they were, she knew she wouldn't be able to keep her mum in the dark much longer - about the baby or the breakup.

She sighed, turning to the window, watching as the city lights blurred. Despite her best efforts to focus on anything else, her thoughts drifted back to Elliot.

Was he thinking about her? Or was he with *her*?

. . .

Across town, Elliot slumped onto a bar stool as the hipster bartender poured him yet another glass of bourbon. The man had a perfectly groomed beard, dark-rimmed glasses and a colourful tattoo winding up his arm. He moved with precision, flipping bottles and wiping the counter with a practiced, almost theatrical flair.

He wasn't even sure why he was here. He could just as easily drink at his mother's house, where he was staying for the time being. Yet here he was, in some trendy bar, wearing a black hoodie he hadn't washed in days, nursing a seemingly bottomless tab.

The moment he walked out Paige's door, he knew he had made the biggest mistake of his life. It wasn't just that she was pregnant - it was that she had so easily let him go. She had told him not to contact her again, and she had meant it. He had pushed her to the point of no return, and the finality of that terrified him.

He was so consumed by the wreckage of their relationship that he had almost forgotten about Heather. Now, even her name made him sick. He didn't know what had drawn him to her in the first place. She was... fine. Decent job, nice enough, unremarkable. Average. She didn't swoon over him like the others; she treated him as an equal. In that, she reminded him of Paige.

But there was one irrefutable difference. He had Paige. And now... he didn't.

Elliot threw his head back, embracing the bourbon's sting as her final words echoed through his mind.

He had her.

Not just physically. Paige had been his constant, his calm in the chaos - the one person who truly saw him. And physically... she had taken him to places he hadn't known existed. With her, everything had felt heightened. Sacred. He remembered reading once that if you were drawn to someone's natural scent, it meant they were your soulmate. He had never doubted it with Paige.

As the alcohol blurred his mind, memories came to the fore - nights tangled in sheets, bathed in moonlight. The silver glow of her skin, the way he'd memorised every curve, every freckle, like scripture. He could still feel the shiver beneath his lips, the catch of her breath as he kissed her slowly, reverently, leaving goosebumps in his wake. The taste of her. The feel of her. God... it undid him.

His hands clenched the glass. His chest ached. Drunk on memory and regret, one truth struck harder than any hangover:

He had her and he had let her go. He had made the biggest mistake of his life.

"What are you doing here, Prince?"

The voice came from behind him, low, amused and unmistakably familiar. Elliot blinked, lifted his head, and spun around, wobbly and ungraceful, to find Shaun standing there with his arms crossed. The nickname tightened something in Elliot's chest. *Prince.* He had called him that for as long as he could remember, insinuating that he had never had to work as hard as others. The nickname was nothing more than a running bit between friends, or at least that is how Elliot had always taken it. A harmless tease, a little zap of competitiveness, nothing deeper.

"Shaun..." Elliot slurred, blinking harder to try and bring the room into focus.

Shaun's brow creased. "Man, how much have you had to drink?"

He didn't bother waiting for an answer. Instead, he slipped an arm around Elliot's shoulders and eased him off the bar stool that had served as his throne for the last few hours. With a tight nod to the bartender, Shaun settled the tab and steered him toward the door.

The crisp New York air hit Elliot like a slap - hard enough to cut through his boozy fog.

"I fucked up, man," Elliot groaned, turning toward Shaun with far too much force, nearly stumbling in the process.

"I know."

The quiet certainty in Shaun's words stopped Elliot cold. "What do you mean, you know?"

"Jess told me." Shaun shrugged - casual. Too casual.

"How the hell would Jess know?"

Shaun raised an eyebrow. "What do you mean, how? You called her last night - off your face - and told her everything. Twice, apparently."

Elliot's mind scrambled, clawing through the liquor-soaked gaps where memories should be. Nothing but blur and static and holes. What day was it?

His stomach twisted. The only routine he had left was simple and vicious - drink, wander, blackout, repeat.

Shaun watched him closely, eyes scanning the damage with the practiced precision of someone who'd done this many times. He had spent hours tracking Elliot down over the years - he always did when things got bad. By now, he knew the patterns. Elliot would go dark, power off his phone and melt into the city's shadows, desperate to outrun the ghosts in his mind.

This time, Shaun had turned to social media. A couple of blurry fan photos had tagged the bar's location and, just like always, Elliot's obsessive following had unwittingly become the clue that led Shaun straight to him. Sometimes, Shaun thought, they were good for something after all.

"My life is over, man," Elliot groaned as Shaun guided him into the back seat of the cab.

He slumped against the window, cheek pressed to the cold glass. The stale smell of the interior hit him, but he didn't flinch. His eyes fluttered shut and, within seconds, exhaustion dragged him under. Shaun watched him from across the back seat, not out of concern but out of habit. Elliot collapsing like this had become routine, almost predictable. There was no part of Shaun that hoped he'd rest or recover - if anything, Elliot falling apart made things easier. Quieter. More controllable. But sleep rarely came for Elliot, not when every time he closed his eyes the weight of his choices pressed in, dragging all those buried demons with them.

Paige

PAIGE SAT down at the dining table she'd eaten at nearly every night of her childhood. She looked around, her smile softening at the familiar chaos around her.

Her siblings, Jasper and Grace, were mid-argument about a hidden message in a TV show they'd been watching, while their mum, Theresa, pottered around the kitchen, insisting - again - that the toaster wasn't broken and did not require her husband's enthusiastic attempts to 'fix' it. It felt exactly like old times.

Jasper, clearly a few drinks in, began theatrically recounting his latest romantic disaster. Paige couldn't help but laugh as he added sound effects and wild hand gestures, re-enacting the moment he'd completely embarrassed himself. The laughter warmed her from the inside out.

This house, this table, this family… it was exactly what she needed.

She glanced at her mum, who was watching her three children with that quiet, unwavering love Paige had known her entire life. And in that moment, Paige wondered if she would look at her own child that way someday? Would she sit at a table like this, with stories and loud laughter, remembering what it felt like to carry that child inside her?

She hoped so.

Paige had been raised by a strong woman, one who had done most of it alone. She was just entering her first years of high school when her stepfather, Lou, came into their lives. While he was there to support her mother through everything the world threw at them, Lou knew he could never simply step into the role of 'dad'.

From the lounge room, the soft sound of snoring drifted in - Lou, asleep in his recliner, the television murmuring some daytime soap in the background. The familiar hum of the house, the clink of dishes in the sink, the delicious aroma of cooked steak lingering in the air - all surrounded Paige like a blanket.

How could she create memories like this for her child?

Silently, she stood and began clearing the plates, stacking them in the chipped ceramic sink. The countertops were still scattered with crumbs and wet tea towels. She wiped them clean, turning her back to the table to hide the tears threatening to spill. The soft tick of the wall clock felt louder than usual in the quiet kitchen.

"How are you, P?"

Theresa's voice came from behind, gentle and steady, startling Paige slightly. As her mother stepped into the room carrying the last of the dishes, she caught a faint whiff of lavender soap, the fragrance of home.

"Yeah, good. How about you?" Paige replied, lying without thinking.

Theresa studied her daughter's face, searching for the source of the tiredness and distant expression. "Want to tell me what's going on?" she asked softly. The question cracked something open.

Paige broke down, sobs ripping through her in waves. Without hesitation, Theresa stepped forward and wrapped her arms around her, rubbing her back like she had done countless times before. She whispered soft, soothing words into Paige's ear - the same way she had when she was little, when scraped knees or nightmares had left her shaking. The warmth of her mother's body anchored Paige in the moment, even as the tears continued to fall.

Though Paige couldn't see it, her mother's heart was quietly breaking, splintering into painful pieces as she held her firstborn and felt her pain.

"I don't know what to do," Paige sobbed, her voice cracking.

"About what, honey? The baby?"

Paige froze, pulling back with tear-streaked cheeks, her breath catching.

Theresa's lips curved into a soft, knowing smile. "Oh, please. Did you really think you could hide something like that from me?"

Her musical laugh carried through the kitchen, lifting just a little of the weight from Paige's chest. "I've been pregnant twice - with three humans. I know a baby bump when I see one. And no amount of baggy jumpers is going to fool these eagle eyes."

Paige's gaze flicked up. Jasper leaned against the counter, arms crossed, his brow furrowed with concern. Grace hovered near the sink, shifting from foot to foot, as if unsure whether to speak or step back. A pang of guilt stabbed her chest. She was supposed to be the strong one, the protector.

From the moment their mum brought the twins home, Paige had felt the bond that would become the backbone of their family. Only a few years older than them, she had instantly claimed them as her babies. Like a guard dog in pigtails, she had vigilantly watched the babies, suspicious of anyone who approached them. As they grew, the three of them fell into a rhythm only siblings could understand. They fought over bathroom time, stole each other's food and traded insults like currency, all the while knowing that beneath the chaos was something unshakeable, something that would never break.

Now Paige was about to bring someone new into that circle, someone who would change the rhythm of their lives, forever. Her shoulders ached with stress but, as she looked at her brother and sister, their expressions a mix of worry, love and quiet trust, she felt a small spark of hope. Maybe, somehow, they would figure this out together, just like they always had.

With that, the floodgates opened. Paige spoke freely, leaving nothing untouched - her pregnancy, the stress of her new book, the breakup with Elliot and his new 'friend', Heather. Her family listened, hanging on every word, their expressions shifting from shock to horror to anger as the week's events unfolded.

When she finished, there was silence. Jasper finally broke it, exclaiming, "What the hell?!" Grace followed, outraged on her sister's behalf. Theresa tried to offer perspective, suggesting the relationship was rooted in their professional relationship and, when that was howled down, she hinted he might be confused or not himself. All three of her children turned to look at her, speechless.

"What are you going to do, Paige?" Grace asked softly, her voice laced with love and fear.

Paige exhaled slowly, shoulder sagging. "I don't know. All I know is… I'm having a baby. And in a couple of months, my book comes out." She shrugged, trying to make it simpler than it felt.

Grace nodded. "One step at a time."

They began clearing the dishes together, slipping into small talk as they reset the kitchen. Their breezy chatter lightened the air. Afterwards, Paige hesitated. "Is it okay if I stay the night? I just… I don't want to be alone in my apartment."

"Of course," Theresa said instantly. "I'll make up your old room."

Grace grinned. "You know we're always here for you P. Whatever you need!"

"Absolutely!" Jasper added, smiling. "I can't believe I'm about to have a little niece or nephew."

PAIGE MOVED UPSTAIRS, her fingers gliding along the bannister, the grooves of the wood so familiar to her touch. Reaching her childhood bedroom, she stepped through the doorway and marvelled at the way time had stood still, preserving memories she had long forgotten. The shabby bookshelf to her left was full of her favourite books; old friends whose words had influenced her destiny, their covers shiny yet worn. On her old timber desk and along the ornamental wall shelves sat numerous trophies and awards, long forgotten reminders of the young girl she used to be - a prize-winning gymnast, spelling champ and editor of the school newspaper who dreamed about writing a book. It was a room that remembered the girl she used to be; a girl she had forgotten.

As she lay on her bed engulfed in the past, a gentle knock at the door and soft footfalls drew her into the present. Her mother lowered herself onto the bed, drawing the woollen blankets up to cover them both. Clasping her daughter tightly in a way that said more than words ever could, Theresa whispered, "Are you scared?"

"Yes… and no." Paige shrugged, her voice barely audible. "I'm not sure what the future holds. I'm not even sure I'll be good at this whole parenting thing."

Theresa searched out Paige's hand. "I can promise you - you will be."

She paused, her thumb brushing over Paige's knuckles.

"Do you remember much from when your father left?"

"Bits and pieces. Not much, though." Paige shook her head.

"Hmm. I guess you were only ten. Well…" Theresa sighed softly. "Let me tell you a little secret. I honestly didn't see it coming. I thought he was going next door just to be neighbourly, you know, fix a few things; lend a hand. I didn't think he was going there with… ulterior motives." Theresa's eyes glazed as she spoke, memories clearly pulling her somewhere far away.

"When he left, I felt broken for a long while. There were nights I'd put you three to bed, then climb into my wardrobe, sit on the floor and just cry."

"Really? Why the wardrobe of all places?" Paige tried to hide a smile at the image, but failed.

Theresa let out a dry laugh and looked down at the corner of the blanket in her hands, picking at a loose thread that had caught her eye. "I didn't want you to see me break."

The silence between them was thick but comforting, and Theresa went on.

"I felt like I had to protect you. I didn't want to confuse you or have you ask questions I couldn't answer. I'd already told you about my plans to renew our vows; to surprise the family with a trip to Hawaii. Maybe, deep down, I knew something was wrong. Maybe that was me overcompensating.

"Anyway…" she exhaled slowly. "What I'm trying to say is, I didn't want those moments to be what you remembered about your childhood. I fell apart in silence so I could protect your memories of him. I made that decision for myself. I made it because I felt that was what I needed to do in my situation."

The similarities between their situations was not lost on Paige. Theresa gave her hand a firmer squeeze. "You don't need to decide what to do about Elliot right now. Take all the time you need and trust your instincts. Whatever choice you make, it'll be the right one."

Her words washed over Paige like a warm tide, filling her with strength.

But just as quickly, something shifted.

Theresa's brows creased. "What's wrong?"

Paige blinked, wide-eyed, a strange look on her face. "I… I think I just felt the baby move."

Her hand trembled as it slid across her belly, pausing where the faint flutter pulsed again - a tiny, private greeting. Tears blurred her vision, spilling quietly as she treasured the moment. It was just her and her baby.

Yes, the road ahead was uncertain. Yes, there were still difficult choices to be made.

But for now, nothing else mattered.

For now, Paige was simply a mother, sitting in the stillness of the night, savouring the first quiet hello from the life growing inside her.

CHAPTER FOUR

Dear little love,

Today, I bought you your first outfit. I wasn't planning to, but somehow I found myself wandering the aisles of Target, letting the world blur around me, letting myself imagine you just a little. And then I saw it.

It was on the sale rack - I hope you won't mind. A tiny Winnie the Pooh costume, soft and golden, like a little hug waiting for you. The moment I held it in my hands, I knew it had been made for you.

I thought about how small you'll be, how your little fingers will curl around mine, how I'll wrap you in this and sing you the same lullabies my mum used to sing me. Soon it will feel like you've been here forever, even though we've only just begun.

I can't wait to meet you, to hold you, to start this life together.

Love,
Mumma

Elliot

Elliot sat on the edge of the couch, spinning a cold bottle cap between his fingers - the kind he picked up on nights when the bar blurred into nothing, when everything felt empty. The vacuum droned in the next room, gnawing at his temples. He pressed his hands against his face, trying to block it out, but it only made the pressure in his skull worse.

Two long strides brought him to the door and he slammed it shut, locking it with a practiced click. Fewer witnesses meant fewer distractions. Fewer witnesses meant fewer lies later. He had run through this conversation a thousand times in his mind, each version more hollow than the last.

His thumb floated over the name on the screen.

Heather.

He braced himself, pressed the smooth glass, and lifted the phone. His stomach rolled. The first ring felt like a drumbeat inside his brain; the second like an echo of every bad decision he'd ever made. By the third ring, his insides had twisted into an unforgiving knot. There was no going back.

"Hello?" The voice that had once felt like an angel's song now grated his ears like nails on a chalkboard.

"Hey, Heather. How's it going?" he said, hoping he sounded cool and collected, even if it was far from the truth.

"Hey, good... sorry, who is this?" The question took him aback as he stammered out his name in a desperate, awkward scramble for control.

"Oh, hey," she said flatly, her tone distant, clipped. "What's up?"

"I… uh…just wanted to let you know I need to take a step back. I can't… do this anymore." The words felt heavy, but speaking them eased the pressure in his chest just a fraction.

"Oh shoot! Did we have plans?"

"Well… no," he muttered.

"Right… so what exactly are you stepping back from?" Her voice was tinged with a hint of laughter and, somewhere behind it, he could hear the murmur of other voices. For a moment, he pictured her surrounded by friends, laughing at him.

"I… never mind. I think I just… got a bit mixed up."

Before she could respond, he ended the call, gripping the phone like a lifeline, trying to salvage the last shred of his dignity.

Paige

Soft moonlight slipped through the white lace curtains of Paige's bedroom window, casting delicate patterns on the wall. The low rumble of traffic drifted up from the street below, a constant, restless sound she'd grown used to.

She'd savoured the time at her mum's house; the brief escape from her new reality. Now, back in the apartment she called home, that comfort had dissipated.

Her thoughts spun restlessly. She tried to calm her breathing, letting the sounds of the city steady her. The hum of tyres, the distant rumble of a bus, the soft, sleepless undertones of a city that never truly sleeps.

A cool breeze slipped through the curtain and brushed across her skin. She placed her hands over her belly, embracing the soft kicks of her unborn child. Each gentle nudge tugged her deeper into the fears she'd been pushing aside.

Would Elliot want to be involved? Would he care enough to try? Had she already taken away her child's chance at a complete family?

Maybe they could co-parent. The thought felt fragile, uncertain. It wouldn't be easy - not after everything that had happened - but maybe it was the right thing. The best thing she could offer her baby.

She didn't know how it would work. She didn't know where to start. But she knew she had to try.

Rolling onto her side, Paige glanced at the clock.

2:00 a.m.

The glowing numerals stared back at her, mocked her. Too late to send a message. Too late to show up at his door with a life-altering question. Too late for another argument. Some things were better said in daylight.

Still, making a decision - even a small one - brought a sliver of relief. The storm in her chest loosened. Her breathing slowed. And finally, sleep pulled her under - still and dreamless.

THE NEXT MORNING, Paige sat on the edge of her bed, staring at her phone as nerves bubbled in her stomach. What was she supposed to say?

Hey, remember how I told you to stay out of our lives? Changed my mind - congratulations, you're a dad!

Right. That would definitely go over well. Her chest tightened at the thought of hearing his voice again. Worse, what if it wasn't his voice she heard? She'd picked up Elliot's phone countless times when he was busy or asleep. Would Heather do the same? Hearing a woman's voice - her voice - on Elliot's phone would shatter her. What if she gloated? What if she twisted this into something cruel; used the baby as a weapon?

Paige dropped her head into her hands, groaning as imaginary headlines flashed through her mind.

Fiction vs. Reality: Paige Lawson Writes Happy Endings, Lives Tragic Ones

A single tear slipped down her cheek; she wiped it away quickly. There was no time for this.

Since walking away from Elliot, Paige had been waging an invisible internal war. Her love for him hadn't disappeared; it still clung stubbornly to the corners of her heart, but anger was starting to seep in. Slowly, betrayal was souring the memories she used to treasure.

And with so many questions left unanswered, she had no idea how to move forward.

If this had been anyone else - any other breakup - Paige would've grabbed her friends, ordered cocktails, and danced the pain away under neon lights. But not now. Not when she was growing a human inside her.

Her normal routines had slipped away too. No more weekend markets, no more Sunday crossword, even doing the laundry on a boring Tuesday night was off limits because she couldn't face the activities, mundane as they might be, that were tainted by recollections of Elliot.

The truth was simple: she didn't know how to respond to these memories because she didn't know how to respond to *him*. After everything he had done - the lies, the affair, choosing someone else - she'd told him to go away and stay gone. So why did she feel like the one who had to fix things?

She had been the one to scream. She had been the one to slam the door. She was the one keeping him from his child.

Yet every decision she made seemed to revolve around how he might feel. Was she protecting him? Excusing him? Letting his emotions matter more than her own?

The realisation hit hard; just like that the haze lifted and she saw the truth. She had been trying to shield the man who had shattered her.... even now, while pregnant and hurting. Her spiral was broken by a sharp knock at the door.

She flinched. No one was supposed to come by.

Heart pounding, Paige stood and padded toward the door, pausing at the barrier that separated her safe haven from the outside world.

She leaned forward and looked through the peephole. She froze.

Shaun Grayson.

One of Elliot's closest friends.

Standing on her doormat.

Her breath caught. Curiosity flared - but so did caution.

Paige opened the door slowly, stepping into the frame with a guarded look, a single unspoken question in her eyes.

"Hi..." she croaked, the word scraping out of her throat.

"We need to talk," Shaun said, his voice cold.

Before she could respond, he brushed past her, stepping into the apartment like he had a hundred times before. But this time something felt different. Any hint of warmth was gone. His presence felt heavier, edged with something hard.

Paige closed the door, her stomach tightening as she followed him to the living room, her bare feet brushing the cool hardwood floor.

Shaun had already taken a seat on the couch. His body was relaxed, but his eyes weren't. They were cold, looking straight through her.

Heat crawled up her neck. Suddenly self conscious, she tugged at the hem of her tank top, smoothing it over the curve of her belly. The bump was obvious now - round and real. When she looked up again, Shaun was staring at it too.

He exhaled sharply, dragging his hands over his face.

"So it's true, then?" he muttered.

Paige stiffened. "What's true?" she asked, her voice light with forced innocence.

"Paige," Shaun cut in. "Don't play dumb."

Her hand instinctively drifted to her bump. She nodded and in response, his expression hardened even more.

"So you're pregnant and you don't even have the decency to let the kid's father be in its life?"

The accusation hit like a slap and Paige's throat closed as anxiety flooded through her. She wanted to defend herself, but guilt choked her words. She *had* told Elliot to stay away. That had been her line in the sand. Her silence only fuelled Shaun's rage. His jaw set hard, and something unforgiving flashed across his face as he stood abruptly, finger pointing at her face.

"What the fuck, Paige!" Shaun exploded, his voice ricocheting off the walls. "Are you seriously not going to say anything? Do you know what you've done to him?"

Her knees trembled.

"He's a fucking mess! I spent two hours getting him up off the floor. He loves you more than anything - and you do *this?*"

Each word landed like venom, burning through her. "I know. I'm sorry," she whispered, the apology instinctive and fragile. Shaun scoffed, pacing the room like a man possessed. He needed her to feel Elliot's pain. To hurt the way he was hurting.

"He cheated on me, Shaun," she said, her voice cracking as the truth tore out of her.

The words dropped between them like a grenade.

Shaun froze and his eyes thinned. "No, he didn't. He never slept with her. Nothing happened."

"He told me he loved her," she fired, anger rising within her once again. "Maybe it wasn't physical, maybe it was an emotional affair, but that doesn't mean it wasn't an affair."

Shaun let out a humourless laugh.

"An emotional affair?" he scoffed. "That's the stupidest thing I've ever heard. You blew up his life over nothing. You're keeping his child from him. All he wants is to be in this baby's life."

His words lashed her like a whip. Staring straight into her wide brown eyes, he stepped closer.

"I thought you were better than this. Obviously, I was wrong. You're nothing but a heartless bitch."

The words pierced her.

Before she could react, he turned on his heels and stormed out, slamming the door behind him.

Silence.

Paige stood frozen, arms wrapped tightly around her chest as if she could hold herself together by force alone. Shaun had never yelled at her before. Never looked at her like that, with something akin to hate.

She'd thought she had already hit rock bottom, but this treachery from someone she trusted, was something else. Something deeper.

Now, in the aftermath, all she could feel was blame. Blame for the affair. Blame for the child growing without a father. Blame for the friendships she'd once treasured now turning against her.

But in all the havoc Shaun had brought to her apartment today, one thing stood out - a thread of light in the darkness.

Elliot wanted to be in the baby's life.

And that was something she could fix.

CHAPTER FIVE

Dear little love,

Shaun stopped by today. I won't share the details with you - this is not your burden - suffice to say it has rattled me and left me with my thoughts all askew. As much as his words hurt - and they did, they cut to my core - it was his manner, his coldness and anger towards me, that rattled me most. I've seen hints of this behaviour over the years, where he has exaggerated perceived ills into something catastrophic, but it's never usually been directed at me. Just your father.

Now that I think about it, I think Shaun has always been jealous of your father. Every time your father got a role, Shaun would pick holes in the storyline or find a flaw in the way he developed his character - for his own good, of course, because he wanted Elliot to be the best he could be. If your father snorted when he laughed, Shaun would mimic him - because that's what friends do, lovingly make fun of each other. If your father revealed his vulnerability, Shaun would later throw it back in his face, using humour to detract from the disloyalty. Over and over again. Yet we never saw it for what it was - betrayal of a friendship.

Sadly, your father always leaned into it, laughed along, always tried harder to impress Shaun. For some reason I still don't understand, Shaun's approval mattered.

I don't want that for you, my little love. I want you to know that you are enough - just the way you are. I'll spend my whole life reminding you that you're worthy, wanted and wonderful. I will always have your back.

Love,
Mumma

Elliot

Elliot sat cross-legged in his mother's old shower, his head held loosely in his hands. Fully clothed, his old red t-shirt and shorts clung tightly to the outline of his body, their weight a comforting presence. Hot steam swirled thickly around him, condensation settling heavily on the glass showerscreen and the mosaic-tiled walls.

The scalding water pricked his skin, marking it with raw red burns. But he didn't mind. The heat soothed him; the warmth of the boiling water penetrating his bones and making its way to his soul in the way nothing else had this past month. He welcomed the reprieve from the numbness that had settled within him. Here, under the pulsating water, he could actually feel. He felt alive.

It had been twenty eight days since that night on the sidewalk. Twenty eight days since he'd destroyed the best thing he'd ever had.

He hadn't slept properly in all that time. Sure, he'd gone to bed and closed his eyes but, no matter how hard he tried, sleep - real sleep - eluded him. Instead, his mind remained a non-stop loop of memories that gave his subconscious no reprieve. The only thing that offered him temporary grace was drinking, and the only person who noticed was his mother. Rosa had always noticed. Sometimes she knew him better than he knew herself.

"What are you doing to yourself, figlio mio?" she asked quizzically.

Without skipping a beat he looked at her, glassy eyed, and said, "I drink because I have things I'm trying to kill inside me."

Now, she stood outside the shower, trying to make out the shape of her beloved only child amidst the billowing steam while he took the brunt of the boiling water like penance. She no longer recognised him. The quietly confident boy with a cheeky grin who had once filled the house with laughter and mischief had become a stranger, a shadow of his former self. Aloof and withdrawn. Rosa had done everything she could think of to connect with her son, to bring him back into the light, but now, unwillingly, she had to admit she had exhausted all options. Except for one.

Paige.

Every time she brought up her name, Elliot shut down or lashed out; her name a catalyst for a maelstrom of emotions. Rosa wasn't scared for herself. She feared for her son. With each passing day, she watched what was left of his soul evaporate.

Enough! Sliding the showerscreen to the left, she reached in and turned off the tap. The torrent stopped midstream, leaving silence and a hazy fog of warm steam. She held out a towel, her voice muted and reassuring.

"Vieni qui, figlio mio."

The tender words broke through Elliot's haze and he looked up, eyes rimmed red. He tried to stand, but the aftermath of his latest bender had rendered his body even more sluggish. Slow and wobbly, he clumsily stumbled forward into her arms.

The moment she wrapped him in the towel and her embrace, he broke. Sobs burst from him - ugly, loud and uncontrolled. Rosa clutched him fiercely, long and hard, willing him a lifeline that would save him from the darkness that threatened to envelop him whole. Whispering supportive words, she steered him to his room, dressed him and fed him; the fragrant minestrone warming him up from the inside. As he ate, she sat pensively by his side, not saying a word. But when Elliot finally spoke, it poured out.

Every mistake. Every fear. Every ache. He told her about the street, the look on Paige's face when he told her about Heather, the silence that followed, the baby. He shakily confided about the drinking, the guilt, the confusion - nothing was left unsaid. Rosa felt each word cut deeper than the last, absorbing his confession in an effort to absolve him of his pain.

As his mind began to clear, he knew, without question, that he was the one to blame. What he still didn't know was why.

"Why did you do it, Elio? I thought you loved her."

The straightforward question landed like a slap. Rosa's voice was subdued, but the weight behind it burned deeper than anything Elliot had felt in weeks. He had been torturing himself, searching for answers in the bottom of every bourbon bottle he could find, and still the truth escaped him.

"I don't know, Ma. Things were good; perfect even." He raked his hands down his face, defeated.

Reflecting on that night in the street, he realised something sickening: the memories he'd tried to romanticise with Heather were not even hers. They were Paige's. Every moment that had been real, felt real, had been with the woman he discarded. "This other woman," Rosa said carefully, "have you pursued her?"

"No. I don't want to," he shrugged.

"Why not? Because of the baby or because you know you made a mistake?"

Still stunned by the idea that he was going to be a father, Elliot stared down at the floor. Rosa was, of course, focused on him, on his healing, but he could feel hints of excitement bubbling just beneath her concern. A baby for Elliot meant a grandchild for Rosa.

"I knew I messed up before I even knew about the baby," he admitted. "I don't know why I was attracted to Heather. I have no idea why I said I loved her. We haven't spoken since the movie ended and, honestly, I'm glad about that."

He rubbed the back of his neck, the shame dragging on his tense muscles. His drunken stupor had cleared, and now the reality was slicing him open with sobering precision.

"Then what do you want?"

"I want her. I want to be there with my family." His voice quavered. "I've already missed so much. I don't want to miss another second, but I think I've done too much damage. I don't think we can come back from this."

As he choked out the words, tears welled in his eyes. He wasn't sure he'd ever feel happiness again but, if there was even the smallest chance she'd speak to him - just once - he'd take it. Even if it was to say goodbye.

"I think you need to talk to someone, amore mio," Rosa said with a lump in her throat.

"I think I do too."

Elliot's phone buzzed against his leg, interrupting his thoughts. He glanced at the screen.

Shaun.

He mouthed a quick sorry to his mother and stepped out into the hallway, answering the call.

"Hello?"

"Hey, Prince. How you going?"

"I've been better." He kept his tone flat.

"Yeah, I get that, man. Just wanted to let you know that I talked to that bitch of an ex-girlfriend of yours…"

Shaun's words stung. Elliot immediately felt his jaw lock and anger surge through his veins.

"What the fuck, Shaun? She's not a bitch."

"Yeah, she is, man. You should've heard her. Went off on this rant about how you ruined her life; how you're a terrible human being. I had to calm her down, tell her she was being inappropriate. I only went over there to try and help fix things, but she wasn't having it. Threw me out before I could finish."

Elliot blinked, stunned. That sure didn't sound like Paige, but then again, she had changed. She had screamed at him. Told him to stay away. Threw him out of their apartment. His chest ached as the seed of doubt Shaun was planting began to sprout.

"She wouldn't do that," Elliot murmured half-heartedly, his tone betraying the lie.

"She threatened to sue you for child support, man. Said she was keeping the kid from you; that you didn't deserve to know it. I swear, she was off the rails."

Shaun's calm voice belied the manipulation and manoeuvring that underpinned his words. He didn't care about the truth, only control. He was a chessmaster who played people like chess pieces, always two steps ahead. Watching others crumble fed his self-importance; giving him the power he so desperately craved. He was enjoying this. Every fire and explosion starts with a spark - like always, Shaun made sure he was the one holding the match.

Elliot broke down as the call ended, Shaun's words echoing like a death sentence in his ears. The thought that he might never see Paige again and never hold the child they had created in love, shattered him. He was a man with nothing left to give.

Always a sensitive soul, Elliot was introspective and emotionally attuned. Yet in the space of a month, everything he had worked so hard to build had collapsed. The lies, the guilt and the silence had undone him completely.

Phone still in hand, Elliot sank to the floor, hugging his knees to his chest as wave after wave of tears wracked his frame. Full-bodied, gutteral, soul-torn sobs; ancient and primal. The kind from which you never fully recover.

And that's where he lay.

A man undone.

On the other side of the room, Rosa stood frozen. Her son was on the precipice of a cliff, a yawning chasm before him. With sorrow propelling him forward, she wanted to snatch him back; pull him away from the edge of grief. But this… this was beyond her.

She reached for her phone with trepidation and dialled a number she knew all too well. She didn't know what she would say. She only knew she had to try.

CHAPTER SIX

Dear little love,

When I was little I used to listen to my mum, your grandma, talk about the way she loved us, how it was different, how it could be overwhelming and sometimes even frustrating. I remember thinking, different from what? How can love be frustrating? I get it now.

This is a different kind of love. It lives in every fibre of me, a piece I never knew was missing. It's fierce and wild at the same time; terrifying in its intensity, but giving me a courage I didn't know I had.

One day, we'll sit and watch The Grinch and I'll point out the scene where his heart triples in size. I'll explain that that's not just make-believe; that it actually happens in real life, because that's what happened when I learnt about you. My grandmother, my Gampsie, used *to tell me she fell in love with me before she met me. I know what she meant now.*

I love you dearly, little one, and as much as I love you now, I know my love for you will grow even more - constant and forever - when I first hold you in my arms.

I still love your father. The love we shared will always be a core part of my essence, but I realise now that he's no longer the nexus of my life. The light in my life has shifted. You are the light now.

Love,

Mumma

Paige

The phone call was expected. The conversation was not.

Paige had presumed that at some point, Elliot would tell his mother about the baby. However, what she hadn't expected was Rosa, her voice weak and faint, begging her to come see him.

Hearing that he was merely a shell of the man he once was both warmed and broke Paige's heart. The anguish he had caused, his infidelity, manifested itself in her nightly ritual of broken sleep. But despite it all, despite the way he had torn her apart, she still loved him. And she hated herself for it. She didn't need Elliot to be her protector or for financial help. She needed him like she needed oxygen - to sustain her heart, body and spirit. He was simply part of her.

There had been many a night when sleep was not forthcoming. Instead she had lain awake for hours on end, watching his glorious chest rise and fall with every breath, tracing his full, seductive lips with her finger, drinking in his classical good looks. She used to lie there, thanking the goddesses in all their splendour for guiding her to her soulmate.

But even then, even when everything was perfect, she knew the truth: a lifetime wouldn't be enough.

And maybe that was what hurt the most. He had promised her a lifetime of love, passion and companionship. He had pledged himself to her more times than she could count.

Now…

How could she ever trust him again? How could she ever trust anyone?

Before she could make sense of her emotions, Paige found herself standing outside the apartment of the woman she had once considered her second mother. Her heart was hammering against her ribs in a frenzy as she stared at the paint-chipped door, deliberating her next actions.

Once Rosa had whispered, "He needs you," she had thrown on the first clothes she could find and rushed over. Taken straight from the dirty pile of clothes on the floor was a large jacket, which not only served to keep her warm, but fortuitously also hid her growing belly. She had moved faster than she had in weeks, and now, standing outside Rosa's home, she realised she needed a moment.

To catch her breath.

To steady herself.

Thoughts swirled chaotically in her head as Paige debated whether she was doing the right thing. The decision to reach out to Elliot to offer him the chance to be there for the baby had been made well before his mother's phone call. But now that she was here, could she actually go through with it?

Anxious and unsure, she took a deep breath, lifted her hand and knocked before her courage abated. A few seconds later the door opened, worry etched into every line of the older woman's face as she welcomed her in.

"Thank you for coming, tesoro," Rosa said with a little smile. "He's in his old room."

The nickname, once a treasured term of endearment that spoke to the closeness of their relationship, now tugged painfully at Paige's heart.

Briefly, she considered hugging Rosa, and then thought better of it. She didn't know where she stood anymore; didn't know if Rosa's opinion of her had changed in the last few weeks. If it had, Paige didn't know if she could cope.

She simply nodded and stepped inside, the familiar vanilla and pomegranate perfume hitting her immediately. Previously, the scent had felt like home; now it turned her stomach, the tiny life growing inside her voicing its own protest.

Funny how even something so beloved could turn on you.

Paige moved carefully through the apartment she had once known like her own, her footsteps soft, unsure.

She stopped outside the open door of Elliot's childhood bedroom and the smell that hit her next made her stomach turn for an entirely different reason.

Bourbon.

Stale cigarettes.

He had been on a binge.

Her eyes scanned the room and landed on the dishevelled form of her ex-lover. His tousled hair was still damp, likely from the shower his mother had forced him to take, and his unkempt beard was in desperate need of a trim.

His rumpled state stunned her. She was struck by the absence of any longing tug; their passionate, emotional connection seemingly broken. Why did she not feel anything?

Their eyes locked. Tentatively searching his face for longed-for answers, Paige frantically tried to make sense of this new reality. Elliot, meanwhile, was struck by her presence in his room, seemingly committing her visage to memory in case this encounter should be their last. "Paige?" he rasped.

She was exactly as he remembered her, still so achingly beautiful. Her glossy hair tumbled over her shoulders, random curls sun-kissed with natural gold or auburn highlights. Her alabaster skin sparkled despite the dark circles that had settled underneath her eyes, telling her own story of misery. Immediately - instinctively - his pulse kicked into overdrive. He wanted her. He wanted her back.

But he couldn't move. His words caught in his dry throat.

"Your mum rang me..." Paige started, before trailing off, the heavy silence between them suffocating her.

"You both need to talk," Rosa said firmly, her voice brooking no argument. "You need to work things out or come to a mutual agreement. I will not have my grandbaby brought into a situation like this."

"Do...do you want to sit down?" Elliot stuttered, motioning awkwardly to the bed as he stood.

Paige shook her head. "No. Thank you. I'll stand."

Rosa, not having it, gave her an insistent nudge. "No, you will sit down. Now talk."

And with that, the woman Paige admired so fiercely swept out of the room, closing the door with finality, leaving an uncomfortable silence in her wake.

The tension in the room was palpable. It settled over them like a blanket causing Paige to shift uncomfortably, a rising warmth suffusing her body. Without thinking, she shrugged off the oversized jacket, revealing the fitted striped shirt stretched snugly over her growing bump.

Elliot froze. He couldn't take his eyes off her.

The urge to cross the room, to kiss her, to fall at her feet and beg for forgiveness, nearly knocked him off his feet. He wanted to reach out, stroke the curve of her belly and whisper to the life growing inside, but he stayed rooted where he stood, guilt crashing down around him. He hated himself more in that moment than he ever thought possible.

Paige caught him staring and quickly moved to cover herself, his gaze unnerving her.

No. He had given her this child. The baby was not some shameful secret she was going to tuck away. If the sight of her burgeoning bump stirred up feelings of guilt or regret, that was his burden to carry, not hers.

"I'm sorry," Elliot said after what felt like an eternity.

He hung his head, shame radiating off him in waves. He waited for her explosion - the accusations, her cutting words - but it never came. When he finally lifted his eyes, it was worse than he expected. She was glaring at him, emotionless; her stare hard and unyielding

He swallowed hard, her indifference rendering him mute. He didn't blame her one bit, but he didn't know how to move forward; how to reach her.

"What do you want, Elliot?" Her voice was neutral, direct; so cold it made him flinch.

His throat tightened, but he pushed the words out carefully, one at a time. "I want you."

The confession was unexpected. He could see that in the way her eyes flickered, her mind trying to comprehend what he had just said. Sensing her confusion he continued, hoping against hope that he could break through her walls she had put up to protect herself.

"I'm sorry I hurt you. I was stupid. Weak. I don't know why I did what I did. I don't know why I even looked at her when it's always been you."

Paige rolled her eyes, irritated. "You're only saying this because of the baby. You don't have to…you don't have to lie. I've been thinking about it and you should be part of their life. For the baby's sake. Not mine."

"No, it's not just the baby," Elliot continued quickly, desperately. "Part of it is, yes, but it's mostly about you. I want you. I would want you even if there were no baby. I want our life back."

His voice caught, but Paige didn't waiver. She was resolute, standing tall, strong and unshakable. She wasn't interested in apologies or excuses. That time had passed. She had come here solely to let him know he could be a part of the baby's life.

And with a few words she dealt him an almost physical blow. "I'm not interested, Elliot."

Stumbling back, he tried to catch his balance, his arms stretched out in front of him as though defending himself from further verbal blows. "Please, Paige!" he cried out, voice ragged and broken. "Please give me another chance!"

Before she could react, Elliot dropped to his knees in front of her, his arms around her waist; a drowning man clinging to his last hope of survival.

The action stunned her into stillness. Her first instinct was to shove him away - violently, forcefully - but then a small part of her, the part that still remembered the man he used to be, embraced the reminder of happier times and let him be...for a little while.

"I can't," Paige sighed, "I don't trust you."

Elliot lifted his head, his emerald green eyes shimmering as tears silently rolled down his cheeks. Her gaze drifted to his lips, lips once full and tempting, now drained of life. They mouthed voiceless pleas for forgiveness that Paige refused to acknowledge. They didn't tempt her anymore. They only made her sad.

"Please..." Elliot pleaded, his voice raw. "Please let me make this right. I'll do anything."

He dropped his head again, this time staring at the roundness of her belly. Cautiously, haltingly, he lifted his left hand, the question implied. For one long, painful beat, Paige said nothing, before a small nod escaped her. He lowered his hand until it rested lightly against the new fullness.

Warmth radiated through the thin fabric of her shirt, searing her skin. It was electric, an invisible current racing between them - through him, into her and back again. The spark was undeniable. Unaware of what she was doing, Paige held her breath, watching the man who had broken her heart meet the child they had created together, in love.

And then it happened. As if on cue, a short, swift kick thudded against Elliot's hand. He gasped, his whole body freezing as his child acknowledged him for the first time. His mind wandered: wobbly first steps, bubbly giggles, birthdays, scraped knees, proud smiles - these vignettes revealing the joy that lay ahead. A fierce, all-consuming need to protect at all costs flew through him. He was a father. He knew, right then, right there, that he had to step up. He would not allow his child to grow up like he had - abandoned, lost, searching.

Paige, too, felt her own emotions spiral out of control; the sight of him so open, so vulnerable, stimulated something deep and aching within her. For a moment, there were no lies.

No betrayal.

No heartbreak.

Just a man.

A woman.

And the tiny life connecting them.

Paige watched silently as Elliot's hand moved in slow, reverent circles across her belly. His head bowed low, she could just make out murmured apologies and whispered I love yous as he tried to etch himself into the very life growing there.

Slowly, so slowly it almost went unnoticed, something shifted inside her. The walls she had painstakingly crafted around her heart started to fracture, hairline cracks weakening her defences.

She didn't know what the future held. She didn't know if she could ever fully trust Elliot again, nor if what they used to have was worth fighting for. But this much she knew with absolute certainty - she would give him the chance to be the father her baby deserved. No matter what.

CHAPTER SEVEN

Dear little love,

I'm trying. I'm trying so hard.

It's been two weeks since your father and I sat down and had our talk, and boy, it's been an interesting time.

Every morning, he comes by to check on us, bringing us breakfast and a decaf latte because that's all I can stomach these days. Then he runs errands, but still finds time to text me throughout the day. I can see that he's trying to make up for the pain he has caused, but I don't have the energy to dwell on that. I've asked that we don't talk about our relationship; that we keep our focus on you. For the most part, that's working.

We've argued about your room. He wants to paint it pink or blue; the traditional, conventional choices. I want green. Green for growth. For change. For choice. He thinks I'm being silly, but I feel like you deserve the space - figuratively and literally - to choose your own path when you're older; to be the person you want to be. I know the colour of the walls won't actually influence the person you become, but to me it's symbolic of the freedom we are giving you to shine brightly in this world, knowing we will support all your choices.

When we're talking about you like this, sometimes the hurt softens, and my love for him creeps back in. Watching him show his love for you means more than I can actually put into words. I still don't trust him. Not yet. But maybe... one day.

Love,

Mumma

*P*aige closed the leather-bound book, breathing in its distinctive earthy scent. Her sense of smell had gone into overdrive during pregnancy and her love of reading had deepened, drawn now not just to the stories themselves but to the rich, comforting smell of the pages themselves.

After her emotional reunion with Elliot two weeks ago, she had shared the ultrasound pictures with him and Rosa, keeping them abreast of every milestone. Watching Elliot's face light up as he asked questions about the baby made her heart ache. It was as if, with every small kindness, he mended one more fragment of the heart he had shattered. Sure, he still had a long way to go if he ever hoped to rebuild her trust, but at least, for now, he was headed in the right direction.

Rosa had watched it all with misty eyes. She had always worried that Elliot would be too shy, too guarded, too lost in his career to make room for a family. To see this tender, imperfect new beginning unfold felt like a gift.

When Paige had mentioned in passing that she was writing letters to the baby, Rosa had returned the very next day with the leather-bound book now resting in Paige's lap. It was a quiet way of saying: this matters. This is precious. Don't lose a word of it.

The heartfelt gesture touched Paige, who hadn't quite known what to expect from Rosa given recent events. However, her tender hugs and warm smiles spoke volumes. When she whispered how proud she was that Paige would be the mother of her grandchild, Paige had realised just how much she loved her.

She was pulled from her thoughts by a soft touch of a hand on her shoulder. Startled, she looked up to see a pleasant-looking man with fine smile lines looking down at her, his grey eyes kind and friendly.

"Sorry to startle you, Paige. Are you ready for our meeting?" he asked, his perfect teeth flashing as he spoke.

For the briefest of moments, she was caught off guard. Of course, she had met Jason several times before, but that was before everything went down and the world as she knew it exploded. She was a different person now, more guarded when it came to people and their intentions.

She found herself studying the constellation of freckles across his cheeks and the shiny pink scar near his nose. For some reason, her treacherous mind brought up images of Elliot - classically handsome with no imperfections at all. Erggh! She needed to stop that! She hadn't realised she had been staring until he motioned again towards the boardroom, a smile threatening the corners of his mouth. She quickly tucked her book into her bag, adjusted her coat to better hide her bump, and stood.

"Thanks, Jason," she said, offering a small, grateful smile as she made her way into his office.

She took her place at the mahogany table, sinking into one of the oversized leather chairs. Jason sat beside her, and immediately her senses were flooded by the light and intoxicating scent of his cologne. While not unpleasant, the intensity of the smell caused her stomach to roll.

Their meeting went smoothly. They discussed the upcoming press tour and finalised the dates, leaving Paige more confident about the tour, and her career as a whole.

When she had first learned her manager and publicist was planning to retire six months ago, Paige had been nervous about starting afresh with someone new. Together, Robert and Paige had weathered the challenges of the early days of her writing career. With his years of knowledge and industry experience he was her greatest cheerleader, constant and reliable. Not only did he provide invaluable professional assistance to her by acting as a sounding board for her often crazy ideas, he was also a trusted friend, inspiring her to believe in herself and chase her dreams. As much as she admired Robert, when he had assured her that his son would be the right person to look after her moving forward as he took over his father's company, she remained doubtful.

But Jason had surpassed every expectation. Sitting beside him now, she realised just how much she trusted his well-considered counsel. He would be a strong advocate for her as she promoted her latest work, holding her best interests at heart.

Jason insisted on escorting Paige down to the lobby after their meeting. As they reached the glass doors, she turned to him with one final question.

"So, can we keep the pregnancy under wraps a little longer?" she asked, her voice low.

"We'll try," Jason assured her with an easy smile. "I've scheduled all your TV interviews and photoshoots for the next few weeks. By the time the bump is more obvious, you'll mostly be doing radio interviews. I've already put agreements in place that they won't ask about your personal life unless you open the door."

Relieved, Paige exhaled a soft breath, grateful for his thoroughness. Her bump was definitely on show these days, but beneath her brown trench coat, it was still easily concealed. She silently thanked the universe that she would be pregnant during what people were expecting to be a particularly chilly spring.

"Thank you," she said sincerely, pulling her jacket tighter around her. "With everything still so uncertain with Elliot, I'm just not ready to answer questions."

She glanced around, suddenly noting that Jason had not only walked her to the lobby, but had also stepped outside into the cold to hail her a cab. His kindness was effortless, woven into everything he did. A gentleman through and through, just like his dad.

"I understand," Jason said, stepping aside as a cab slowed to the curb. "Look after yourself, Paige. Until next time…"

He extended his hand towards her in farewell. His grip was steady, offering solace. When she met his grey eyes, she was confident Robert had been right - she and her writing career were in capable hands.

She didn't notice the dark figure lingering across the street, masked by the shadow of the building.

Watching. Waiting.

CHAPTER EIGHT

Dear little love,

I finished my manuscript today. I mean, technically, it had been finished for a while but I just finished my last edit. It's ready; ready to invite the reader on a magical journey of discovery. I guess that's the beautiful thing about fantasy. You might be reading a story about mythical creatures, but the feelings the writing evokes in you are very real.

Writing has always been my escape; a way to hide from the world, share my truth. I don't mind admitting that I sat back and cried when I finished that last sentence - not because I was sad, but because I was proud. There is always an element of pride in my work, don't get me wrong, but to me it's always felt like something was missing, something I could never put my finger on - *je ne sais quoi.* This time it's different; it just feels complete.

Perhaps it's because the final book of my series signifies the start of a new storyline in my own life. It truly feels monumental. You're making me feel whole.

And you know what? Things with your dad feel lighter too. Our journey may have been rocky of late, but the clouds are parting and the sun is starting to peep through. Maybe the hard part's behind us. Maybe everything is starting to fall into place - the way it should be.

Love,

Mumma

Elliot

*E*lliot stood in the middle of the gym, his quads, glutes and hamstrings burning after a vigorous set of squats under his trainer's watchful eye. Hunched over and breathing in short, shallow bursts, he couldn't help but share his news with Dean, a huge grin splitting his face.

"Congratulations, man! Fatherhood is amazing!" Dean enthused, giving him a hearty slap on the shoulder.

"Thanks, man! I'm so excited. Honestly, it's the best thing that's ever happened to me," Elliot beamed, the truth of that statement vibrating through his whole body.

Dean chuckled. "Do you know what you're having yet?"

"No, not yet. We've got a doctor's appointment tomorrow, but I don't know if Paige wants to find out," Elliot admitted, wiping sweat from his forehead.

He had been floating on cloud nine since that night at his mother's house - the night Paige had ever so slightly opened the door he had nearly slammed shut. She was adamant she didn't want to talk about their relationship yet - and he respected that entirely - but sometimes, in quiet moments, it felt like they were slipping back into the familiar. Something he wanted and hadn't dared hope for.

His mind drifted back to the night before.

They'd slipped into an easy routine. He would cook dinner for her, pack the dishwasher and then leave for his mother's house, respecting her privacy and desire for space. Last night, Paige had surprised him as he was preparing to depart.

"Do you want to feel the baby kick?" she had asked shyly, her hand brushing over her stomach.

Sitting side-by-side on the lounge, she directed his hand to her belly. Still amazed at the thought she was carrying his child, Elliot bided his time, waiting patiently.

With a slight smile, she suggested he talk to the baby. Heeding her advice, Elliot leaned down, bringing his face close to the bump and, sweetly out of tune, softly sang an old Italian verse his mother used to sing to him.

The air between them crackled with anticipation and then, there it was - a big, strong kick. A wave of happiness swept over him, its intensity flooding him. Picking up on his cues, Paige let out a giggle, the melodic sound music to his ears. It gave him hope for the future.

Shaking himself out of his reverie, Elliot moved on to his next rotation - deadlifts. Feet planted firmly on the floor, he tightened his core and shakily lifted the steel barbell above his head, his whole body trembling at the exertion required. The weights, although well below what he would normally do, felt so heavy - impossibly heavy. One was all he could manage today.

With the fatigue settling into his bones, he grabbed his towel and trudged to the showers, throwing his gym bag over his shoulder. He pulled out his phone, half expecting, well, hoping really, for a text from Paige. But there was nothing; just a message from Shaun asking if he wanted to grab lunch.

Elliot frowned, typing out a quick reply with a time and place. As he shoved his phone back into his pocket, the words from his previous conversation with Shaun wormed their way back into his brain. The ugly doubts. The accusations. The idea that Paige only wanted him around for child support.

They had shared such a beautiful, intimate moment last night. It couldn't possibly be true. Could it?

Stepping into the restaurant, Elliot's nostrils were assailed by the strong smell of seafood. Scanning the room, his eyes soon found Shaun. With easy steps, he made his way over, pulling Shaun into a brief hug, the oils of his cheap cologne clinging to his clothes. Sliding into the seat across from him, Elliot felt unexpectedly lighter. The conversation flowed freely as they placed their orders and waited for their meals to arrive.

"So…" Shaun began, a casual grin tugging at his mouth. "How's Paige going?"

At the mere mention of her name a bright smile bloomed across Elliot's face. His heart swelled as he leaned forward, unable to hide his excitement.

"She's doing really well - both her and the baby. God, I still can't believe I'm going to be a dad. An actual father!" He giggled softly, the wonder still fresh on his tongue. "It blows my mind every time I think about it. We don't know for sure, but Paige thinks it's a girl. She has this perfect little bump. She says it's huge but, honestly, it's not. And there's this glow about her now - she just lights up the whole room."

Elliot's grin refused to loosen its hold, his words coming faster, pouring out of his mouth. "I never thought it would be possible, but I'm more attracted to her now than I've ever been. She's incredible, Shaun. I just…" He paused, shaking his head, "I love her so much."

Shaun nodded along, half-listening, a polite smile plastered on his face. He waited; waited for the perfect moment to drop the bombshell he had been carefully crafting in his mind. When the time was right, he would strike.

"Oh, so things are good?" Shaun checked, his voice deceptively casual.

"Yeah, man, really good," Elliot confirmed.

"And you two are… seeing each other? Like, actually dating again?"

Elliot hesitated, his smile falling away. "I mean… no. Not dating, exactly. But still together-ish, you know? We're working on things." The half-truth hurt. Knowing they were prioritising their child and not addressing the issues with their relationship - at Paige's request - pained him, but he was so sure that was the logical next step. It was just a matter of time.

The way he shrugged, the twinge of insecurity darting across his face, was all the opening Shaun needed.

"I only ask," Shaun said, his tone indifferent, "because I saw her earlier, getting real cozy with some guy. A couple of hours ago, actually."

Elliot stiffened. The words didn't make sense at first; they were indecipherable. Little by little he took on their meaning, willing himself not to react.

"I thought you two had decided to see other people?" Shaun persisted, hammering his point home. "They were all over each other in the middle of the damn street. I wouldn't be surprised if paparazzi got a few happy snaps. They looked pretty close, if you get my drift."

Elliot's stomach dropped. His heart thudded painfully against his ribs, each beat another blow.

"You, um, what?" Elliot struggled to get words out; coherent thought no longer an option. He could not meet his friend's eyes, afraid that if he did, the tears that hovered just below the surface would not stop.

Shaun shrugged, playing innocent. "Just saying, man. And honestly, are you even sure you're the father? I mean, you've got a lot of money. Maybe you're just the easiest mark."

The words hit Elliot like a punch to the gut. Shaun watched closely, waiting for the inevitable.

There it was.

The light in Elliot's eyes receded, leaving doubt, fear and shame in its wake.

Shaun almost smiled, his lips twitching. He lived for this - the slow, calculated destruction; the devastation no photograph could ever capture. This was true power: the ability to rip someone apart, tear them down, with nothing but carefully chosen words.

"She... she wouldn't do that," Elliot whispered unconvincingly. "I'm the father. I have to be."

Just like that, the fantasy he'd been clinging to shattered. His fragile world - the one where he had a family, a future, love - collapsed. Devastated beyond belief, Elliot pushed back from the table and shuffled unsteadily out of the restaurant, the world closing in around him.

Shaun didn't follow. Instead, he leaned back in his chair, waited for the food to arrive and dug in - satisfied. Breaking Elliot had made him hungry.

Labouring through the streets, Elliot was in a haze, the world around him blurring into insignificance. Cars passed. People hurried by. Cameras clicked. None of it mattered. His mind was a whirlwind, a swirling vortex of emotions with Paige and the baby at the centre.

Could he love a child that might not be his? Did Paige know he was not the baby's father? Why would she do this to him? For revenge? Was she really that cruel?

Jealousy, thick and oppressive, gnawed at his chest, ready to swallow him whole. The idea of a mystery man in Paige's life made his stomach heave - someone else touching her, holding her, being there for the milestones he was supposed to witness. It was too much to bear.

By the time he reached his mother's apartment, Elliot was a shell of himself. He barely spoke; barely moved. He just lay on his bed, staring blankly at the ceiling as Shaun's words poisoned every corner of his mind.

Could she have moved on that quickly? Had he ever really known her at all? And the biggest question of all, played on a loop. Was the baby even his?

Hours slipped by. He didn't know how many. He didn't care. His phone buzzed in his pocket.

Paige.

He stared at her name for a long moment before answering, his voice low and gravelly.

"Hello…"

"Hey, it's me," she said cheerily, her voice giving nothing away. "I didn't hear from you this afternoon. I thought we were having dinner?"

He closed his eyes, guilt slamming into him like a freight train. "Yeah, sorry. Not feeling well. I'm going to sleep," he mumbled, already pulling the phone away from his ear.

But her voice was so sweet, so hopeful, it caught him just before he could hang up. "Will I see you at the doctor's tomorrow?" she asked. Her excitement was undeniable, practically radiating through the line. "We get to see our little baby again!"

Her words wrapped around him like a noose. Our little baby. God, how he wanted it to be true. But the seeds of doubt had already been sown, and they were growing faster than he could kill them.

He couldn't force the words out; couldn't promise her something he wasn't sure about anymore. Cowardly though it was, he did the only thing he could think of. He hung up. The silence that followed was endless.

CHAPTER NINE

Paige

Staring at the phone, Paige silently hoped he would call back, blaming the abrupt end on a lost connection or a clumsy finger. But deep down, she knew better. There had been no accident. No glitch. She racked her brain for anything she might have done or said to trigger this sudden coldness to no avail.

Letting out a sigh, she pulled up the text thread with Elliot and began typing out a message, which she deleted over and over again. What could she even say?

Hi Elliot, I thought things seemed to be going okay with us. What's happened? Are you going to hurt me again?

Paige snorted bitterly to herself. Yeah, that would go down well, especially if the call dropped out because of a poor connection.

Her stomach churned like an angry river, building and building until it was impossible to control. Energy coursed through her veins, frustration and grief catching up all at once. So she did what she did best. She wrote.

Leaning down, she pulled the journal from her bag and let her thoughts flow.

Dear little love,

I don't know what happened.

One minute, your dad and I are doing great - planning things for you, focusing on what's best for you. The next, he's hanging up on me and not even saying if he'll come to your next scan.

I hate being in limbo. I hate feeling like everything is out of my control, like I'm just an unwilling participant in this ridiculous situation with my fate already preordained.

Maybe I am overthinking. Technically he didn't say he wasn't coming. He just said he wasn't feeling well and then hung up. That happens - we're all human - so surely I'm reading too much into it. But what if I'm not?

I can be honest with you because I know you may never read this. I think my anxiety, my over-thinking every little thing, stems from fear. Fear of missing something I should have seen before. Were there signs that he was falling in love with Heather and I just... didn't notice?

He hasn't said if he's seeing anyone else. We've never discussed it.

Honestly, I'm not even sure how I'd feel if he was.

Love,

Mumma

Before Paige closed her eyes on another emotionally tumultuous day, she picked up her phone and typed out one last message.

THE NEXT DAY, sitting alone on a cool plastic chair in the doctor's rooms, Paige fidgeted with the hem of her dress. Waiting for the doctor to make his entrance, the silence pressed heavily against her, each tick of the clock amplifying the ache in her chest.

Elliot hadn't responded to her text, nor had he shown up. She tried to make excuses for him - maybe he was stuck in traffic or couldn't find a park nearby. Maybe he was lost and, being a typical male, was too proud to ask for directions. Who knew?

She did though, deep down. He had changed his mind. He didn't want her. He didn't want the baby.

The realisation sent ripples throughout her body. She mentally scolded herself for being so naive, for giving him the power to hurt her again. The pain was too raw for anger, too deep for tears. She was simply... broken.

The doctor entered the room with a warm smile before she could compose herself fully. Summoning what little strength she had left, she sat up straighter, fixed the front of her dress and patted her hair. If her exterior presented as serene and immaculate, he would never be able to guess at the turmoil inside. This she did for her baby. For her little love.

"Hi, Ms Lawson, you're absolutely glowing! How have you been?"

The doctor's heartfelt greeting was accompanied by a smile that reached all the way to his eyes. Noting the sincerity, the simple action succeeded in easing the tension she hadn't realised she was carrying.

"I'm doing really well, Dr Baker, thank you. How about you?" Paige asked, taking a close look at the man before her.

Dr Baker had a smooth, commanding presence that dominated the room. His athletic build was obvious beneath the slim cut, navy linen shirt he wore under his white coat. Dark, close-cropped curls framed a face that looked as though it should be carved in marble and sitting in a museum. Or on the cover of a magazine, thought Paige; either would result in adoration by the masses, which, quite frankly, was his due.

She didn't even realise she was staring - or that he had been talking - until his hand lightly touched her shoulder, snapping her back to reality. "Sorry, what was that?" she asked, her cheeks suffusing with a rosy glow.

"I said move on to the bed, lean back and pull up your dress so we can check on that little one of yours."

The rich, velvety timbre of his voice sent a shiver down her spine. So enthralled was she by the resonant sound, she didn't actually comprehend the instruction, requiring him to repeat it a second time, this time accompanied by a laugh that sounded like music - rich, effortless and harmonious. Paige shook her head, slightly mortified, and walked to the bed, accepting the small towel he handed her and draping it over her legs before carefully lifting her dress to reveal her bump.

The cold jelly made her start involuntarily, but the irritation faded the moment Dr Baker moved the transducer over her stomach and the most beautiful sight filled the screen. Paige had to physically remember to breathe as she scrutinised the pudgy-looking face of her child. The 3D rendering was so lifelike - she could see the baby's perfect pout and the shape of tiny knuckles in a curled fist, held tight to the chin like a boxer. She watched, mesmerised, deliberately taking mental snapshots so she could relive every single detail later. Next thing she knew, Paige was weeping afresh. The profound love she already felt towards the baby seemed to multiply, becoming all-consuming, unshakeable, so much so that heart could no longer bear it.

Cognisant of her raw response but conscious not to intrude on the highly personal moment, Dr Baker gave her arm a feather-light tap, urging her to take all the time she needed to soak in her little miracle. Although he wasn't aware of the details regarding her relationship with the baby's father, from the little he was able to gauge he rightly sensed it was a complicated situation. He didn't press for details, choosing instead to respect her privacy; his attention fixed on the developing foetus.

Acknowledging his unspoken support, Paige shot him a quick smile and nodded for him to continue, but not before taking another lingering glance at the medic by her side. His focus was absolute, but every so often he would turn to her, lock eyes and give a soft, reas-suring smile that made her heart soar. She glanced down at his hand, steady and sure as it moved the wand across her stomach. No wedding ring. She chuckled silently to herself and, before she could betray what she was thinking, she quickly averted her gaze. When she looked up again, she froze.

The doctor's expression had changed.

His easy manner was gone, his undivided attention now on the screen. His brow wrinkled; his face tightened, a muscle on the left side of his jaw spasming intermittently. His body language had changed so subtly, almost imperceptibly, but to someone like Paige, who had spent her whole life reading between the lines, it was screaming.

Something was wrong.

Blood roared in her ears, her thundering heart beating its own drum. Her lungs refused to draw breath, her mouth dry, as she tried to find a rational explanation for the worst case scenarios that were infiltrating her mind and filling her with terror.

Without saying a word, Dr Baker set down the wand, handed her a towel and asked her to clean herself up. And that was it.

Paige wiped the remaining jelly from her stomach, hastily pulled on her shoes, and sat back down near Dr Baker's desk. For once, she was grateful for the hard plastic chair. Its uncomfortable back pressed into her skin, ensuring her focus. Every nerve in her body tingled, screaming for answers.

Dr Baker watched her, concern etched on his sculpted features. Aware of the impact his next words would have on a new expectant mother, he spoke carefully and thoughtfully.

"Ms Lawson, I don't wish to alarm you," he began, "but during the scan, I was checking the baby's organ development and overall measurements. Mostly, everything looks good. Your baby is measuring around the 50th percentile, which is right where we want them to be."

He allowed his words to settle before continuing, the air in the room shifting.

"But there was one abnormality."

Abnormality. The word rang in Paige's ears like a death knell, and the world seemed to slow.

"It appears the kidneys are quite dilated, the left in particular," he continued gently, "meaning it's not draining properly. The condition is called hydronephrosis. Right now, the size suggests a moderate to severe case."

Paige's hands squeezed the arms of the chair, her knuckles turning white.

"What does that mean?" she asked, a queasy sensation overtaking her.

"It means," Dr Baker said carefully, "that we'll need to monitor you closely for the rest of your pregnancy. If the dilation worsens, we may need to deliver early. After birth, the baby may require surgery to determine the cause and relieve the pressure. The longer the kidney remains enlarged, the higher the risk of losing function and - in the worst case - potentially the kidney itself."

The ground beneath her seemed to disappear. Paige stiffened in disbelief, trying to get her head around the sheer enormity of this news. Not much registered as her body's primal instincts took over and she convulsed into uncontrollable, gut-wrenching sobs, conflicting emotions fighting for dominance within her. Fear, guilt, love.

What had caused this? Was it the stress? The heartbreak? Was it something she had done, or worse, something she hadn't done that had contributed to this? Her poor baby!

Gulping, hiccuping cries escaped her, her body shaking like a leaf in a storm. Try as she might to sniffle her nose into submission, a trickle of snot made its way down her face, perilously close to her open mouth. It was the feeling of a large, warm hand on her back that dragged Paige back to the here and now. In the throes of this delirium, she had forgotten the doctor's presence.

He was sitting beside her, occupying the chair usually reserved for partners. Empathising with her distress, he held her, offering a silent, steady comfort. Not as a doctor. Not out of obligation. But as someone who understood, who cared.

For the first time in a long while, Paige let her barriers down and leaned into someone's arms, ceding control. The release was not instantaneous, just a gradual easing of her sore, tense muscles and a quiet acceptance that she would not be on her own. Even if Elliot did not want to be a part of this child's future, she was surrounded by dedicated medical specialists who, together with her family, would be able to help her on this journey, no matter how difficult it would be. Her crying eased and she wiped her eyes, feeling shy, mindful of the spectacle she had made of herself. Before she could apologise for her behaviour, Dr Baker continued.

"Everything will be okay, Paige. That's the worst possible outcome. There's a real possibility that it could completely resolve itself before she's born…"

He stopped mid sentence, his face blanching as he realised what he had said.

"Sh… she?" Paige repeated, her voice shaking anew.

Dr Baker pulled back, running a hand over his face in frustration. "Shit! I'm sorry. I'm so sorry," he muttered, shaking his head. He was furious at himself for the slip, but also for hugging her in the first place. He had delivered bad news many times in his career, but never like this. Never with this much emotion bleeding through the professional boundary.

Unaware of the ethical dilemma her doctor was facing, Paige's shattered heart cautiously began stitching itself back together with a thread of hope.

A daughter. A little girl.

Wiping her tear-streaked cheeks, Paige sat back and stared out the office window, watching cars pull in and out of the medical centre car park. She had to be strong now. There was no other choice. She had a little girl to protect.

With the ultrasound images in hand and printed information about the diagnosis, Paige left the clinic. Her steps were steadier now, her back straighter, her heart marginally stronger.

The fear was still there, gnawing at her bones, but something bigger was rising to meet it. Resolve. She wasn't just fighting for herself anymore.

Sitting on a bench just outside the clinic doors, Paige pulled out her phone. She found the best picture; the clearest one showing her darling daughter's tiny, perfect face.

With trembling fingers, she typed:

> I don't know why you weren't there but I thought you should still see your daughter's face. Please call me. We need to talk.

She attached the photo and hit send before she could change her mind. Then she sat there, staring at the message, praying for an answer she wasn't even sure she believed would come.

CHAPTER TEN

Dear little love,

Knowing I'm expecting a girl is thrilling. It gives me a point of reference and makes your future more real, more brightly coloured.

I used to wonder about the simple things - your eye colour, your hair. But now my thoughts drift to less frivolous things. Will you be scared of the dark like me? Will you use reading as a way to escape reality or will you shine on a stage like your dad? The idea of the latter frightens me but, if that's where you sparkle, where you find your bliss, I'll be there in the front row every time. Loving you already requires me to be braver than I've ever been and somehow, it's making me find the old me, the person I used to be.

I've also been thinking about traditions. I went to school with a girl who was raised by a single mum, and every few months they'd sit down and watch Gilmore Girls together - a mother and daughter watching a show about a mother and daughter. All with largely absent fathers. Hmmm.

Maybe we could do something like that someday. Our own little ritual. Not Gilmore Girls though. I could never get into it, I'm afraid, but maybe it will mean more with you...

When I was growing up, my mum used to take us on 'date nights'. She used to save hard each month so she could treat us to this special occasion. We'd all dress up in our best clothes and she'd whisk us off for dinner, turning the whole night into an event. She spoiled us rotten, and we loved every second of it.

Now that I'm older, I understand how hard that must have been for her, carving out time for three of us, not just one, and somehow making each of us feel like we had 100 percent of her attention. For those few hours, the noise of the world fell away - the buzz of modern life and teenage angst, as well as the internal monologue that constantly tells us to do more, be better. It was just us. Her and her three little shadows, wrapped in a bubble of love she built with nothing but intention and heart.

I can't wait to do something like that with you.

Love,

Mumma

*S*itting alone in a busy café, Paige cradled a lukewarm coffee between her gloved hands, savouring the forbidden taste of caffeine. She knew she shouldn't be having it, but it was the only thing keeping her going right now. With each sip, the rich bitterness seeped through her, offering a fleeting rush of energy; a small, cruel reminder of what feeling alive used to be like.

It had been two weeks since she had last seen Elliot. Two weeks since the ultrasound that changed everything. She was struggling. A decent night's rest was definitely a thing of the past. Sleep had become a stranger, a luxury she no longer believed she merited. Even when she catnapped for an hour or two, it was broken and restless, haunted by worry. The little kicks she once celebrated with giddy excitement now filled her with trepidation. Every day brought her closer to a future she would face alone.

Her appearance mirrored her unravelling heart. Bulky, shapeless sweaters swamped her frame, her belly no longer visible. Her unwashed hair - six days now - was pulled back into a messy bun, her natural waves all but gone, framing an ashen face hollowed out by a fusion of fatigue, fear and despair. Not to mention a general loss of appetite.

The planned media appearances for her new release had all been cancelled. She knew it could affect sales, but she couldn't bring herself to care. Her dreams, her career - even her daughter's arrival - belonged to a ghost; someone from her past denied entry to paradise and forced to live eternity in the gloomy shadows.

The bell above the café door jingled, snapping her temporarily from dark thoughts. Lifting her heavy head, Paige spotted her mother's familiar figure, wrapped in a scarf to starve off the uncommon chill. She managed a small wave, a poor excuse for a smile tugging weakly at her lips.

Sliding into the seat beside her, Theresa took one look at her daughter and wished she could do something - anything - to lift the burdens she carried. The woman in front of her was a mere shell of the vibrant Paige she knew. This was a woman scarred by grief, drowning in a sea of silent pain without an anchor in sight.

Theresa knew, without a word being spoken, that something had to change.

"How are you, honey?" Theresa poised the question in a deceptively non-committal tone.

"I'm okay," Paige lied, knowing full well her mother could see straight through the facade. Before she could ask, Paige briskly cut her off - "No. I haven't heard from him."

Her voice quivered despite her best efforts. "I've called. I've texted. Nothing. I'm blocked." Incongruously, the statement made her laugh aloud, hysteria rising in her voice. "I even tried Rosa. Same thing. Blocked."

The admission tasted like acid on her tongue. He hadn't just left her, he had erased her.

Theresa's face tensed ever so slightly, her hand twitching as if she wanted to reach out and fix the problem somehow. But she said nothing, only nodded, hiding her own anger carefully behind a mask of calm for her daughter's sake. Before Theresa could launch into her next line of questioning, she noticed her daughter's whole demeanour change - her shoulders stiffened, she lowered her head and inhaled a sharp breath. Someone was approaching.

"Paige! Oh my God! The hermit herself, out in the wild."

A fashionably dressed woman in an expensive tailored pantsuit that highlighted her long, long legs, pointedly stopped at Paige's table, forcing an interaction. Theresa watched Paige force an awkward smile in the woman's direction, clearly wishing the earth would swallow her up whole. Right then. Immediately, if not sooner.

"Hi, Jess." The discomfort in her voice rocked Theresa, who prepared to jump in and rescue her eldest child.

"Where have you been? You just vanished one day. No calls, no messages." Jess's voice was accusatory as she pulled out her phone mid-sentence and tapped out a message, attention already drifting to someone new or more important.

"Yeah... I've just been..."

"You should come to this party I'm throwing next week! Everyone will be there." Jess cut her off, bright but insincere.

"Oh, I don't know..." Paige trailed off, scrambling for an excuse and finding nothing.

"Ha! Classic Paige. Gotta stay in with your books, huh? Bit lonely now without Elliot though."

The jab landed squarely, the unspoken meaning hanging between them like smoke. Before Paige could muster a response, Jess looked up long enough to flash a practiced smile, then turned back to her phone.

"Anyway, gotta run. Some of us actually work for a living."

She cackled at her own joke, heels clicking on the tiles as she strode away, coffee sloshing in her manicured hand.

Theresa exhaled softly and glanced at her daughter, who remained motionless, her pale cheeks blushed pink. "Pay her no mind, P. You've got more grace in your little finger than she has in that entire pantsuit. Now tell me how you're really doing."

With those few simple words, her restraint gave way and everything came rushing out. "I feel like I'm drowning," Paige choked out as the first sob tore free. "Nothing is going right. Nothing."

Tears streamed down her face, hot and unrelenting. "What did I do to deserve this?" she cried, her voice cracking under the weight of months of pain. "My partner leaves me. Humiliates me in public because he wanted someone who didn't even know he existed. Then, just when I find the courage to move forward, I tell him about the baby and he says he wants to be involved. He begs me for forgiveness, swearing he'll stay, and for one stupid, desperate moment, I believe him. I try to forget what he did to me and, for the baby's sake, let him back in and then, then he just vanishes without a trace. Blocks me like I'm nothing. Walks away."

Her hands fisted in her lap as her body shook with rage that had been turned inward for far too long.

"Then the day after he abandons me, I find out our daughter is sick." Her voice broke completely on the last word.

"My daughter. Mine." She pressed her hand protectively against her belly. "And there's nothing I can do to help her. I just have to wait. Hope. Pray. For months."

She drew in another ragged breath, feeling like she was being torn apart from the inside.

"I don't know if I can do this. Being a single mum is one thing, but being a single mum to a sick baby? That's something else. I can't do this, Mum. I can't."

The words hung between them as Paige, spent after her outburst, dissolved into tears. Theresa, about to cry herself, pulled her daughter into a tight embrace, repeating comforting words to soothe her soul.

"Shhh… darling. Everything will be okay. I promise you," Theresa whispered, pulling Paige towards her and hugging her like her own life depended on it. "I'll help you every step of the way, you know that. And not just me. You have two very happy, very eager siblings at home who are ready to rally behind you too."

She drew back just enough to cup Paige's face in her hands, her voice fierce and full of unwavering love.

"You are the strongest, smartest, most powerful woman I have ever had the privilege to know. Every single day, I thank the universe that you're my daughter. I am so proud of you. You can do this, Paige. We can do this."

She held her daughter's gaze, brushing a tear from her cheek with her thumb.

"We don't know exactly what will happen with your little girl but, whatever comes, we'll face it - together. Okay?"

Paige nodded through the fresh tears that clung to her lashes and tried to commit her mother's words to memory. After a long hug, she leaned back and looked at her mother. "I don't know what I would do without you." She sighed.

"Probably be a lot less smart and funny," Theresa mused, which made Paige smile for the first time in days. "You're on your way to meet the twins, aren't you?"

"Yeah, but I think it's only Grace. I doubt Jasper wants to go baby shopping." They shared a further giggle before parting ways, their emotional loads a little lighter.

On the street, Theresa stood rooted to the spot, watching her daughter walk away. Her heart was twisting with a mixture of sorrow and fierce resolve. Enough was enough.

She pulled out her phone and quickly dialed. "Hey Gloria, it's Theresa," she said, forcing a calm tone. "I'm so sorry, but I won't be back in the office today. Can you cancel my meetings? No, no, everything's fine, I just have something I need to fix."

There was a pause as Gloria responded, but Theresa was already waving down a cab. "Thanks, Gloria. I'll see you tomorrow."

Ending the call, Theresa tucked the phone into her coat pocket. Her eyes blazed with purpose.

She had something to fix. And it couldn't wait.

Theresa

Standing in front of the apartment door, Theresa readied herself for what she knew would be a battle. Squaring her shoulders, she knocked twice, bracing for the storm to come.

The door swung open, revealing Rosa, her expression a blend of shock and thinly veiled anger at the interloper who dared trespass on their property.

"Theresa? What are you doing here?" Rosa asked, her inflection clipped and cold.

"I'm here to find out why your son deserted my daughter when she needs him most," Theresa growled, pushing her way into the apartment without waiting for an invitation.

"My son did not desert her!" Rosa snapped back. "She was the one trying to rope him into something he didn't want!"

"Rope him into something?" Theresa barked a disbelieving laugh. "What the hell are you talking about? He deserted the mother of his child like the spineless weasel he is! Where is he? I've got a few choice words for him."

"She is not the mother of his child," Rosa hissed, her words sharp enough to cut glass. "She's pregnant with another man's baby, trying to pass it off as Elio's for the money, like the snake she is."

Theresa let out a humourless laugh, folding her arms tightly across her chest.

"Another man's baby? I wish it were another man's baby! Unfortunately, your precious son is the father of my granddaughter and, despite how much I might wish otherwise, that's the truth. And the coward that he is, he's now bailed on both of them when they need him the most."

"Elio told me it was someone else's child," Rosa said, the conviction in her voice faltering ever so slightly.

"He wouldn't lie."

"Are you kidding me?" Theresa shot back.

"Have you met Paige? You remember how she was around Elliot? That girl worshipped the ground he walked on. She loved him like no one else ever could. Come on, Rosa, you know as well as I do that Paige is not that kind of person."

She let the words hang between them, watching as Rosa's face slowly registered their veracity. Theresa knew she had struck the first blow.

"Elio wouldn't lie about something like this," Rosa said, her voice thin and defensive, still holding her ground, not ready to concede victory yet. "He became a different person after he separated from her - so angry, withdrawn. I was relieved when he got that new job and moved to Paris."

She dropped onto the lounge behind her with a heavy sigh, exhausted. With that one movement, the floodgates burst open and Rosa revealed everything that had occurred in the past few weeks.

She told Theresa how Elliot had come home crying, broken-hearted after 'discovering' the baby wasn't his; how he had claimed

Paige was only using him for his money. After lengthy discussions with his mum, Elliot decided the real father was Paige's new publicist, the man Shaun had described seeing her with.

That revelation had crushed Elliot's remaining spirit, filling him with a vile bitterness that threatened to consume him whole. From that moment on, Elliot was a changed man. He stopped caring who he hurt. He drank heavily. He started fights with strangers in bars, exploding at the merest slight. When he wasn't provoking people, he was out with Shaun, growing more and more volatile by the day - a ticking time bomb primed to detonate.

Theresa listened in stunned silence, her heart sinking at Rosa's words. This wasn't the Elliot she had known. This wasn't the man her daughter had loved. Where had it all gone so wrong?

Now, armed with this additional information, Theresa's instincts told her there was still more to uncover. Much more.

"You need to call him and convince him that the baby is his, and that he needs to come home right now!" Theresa demanded, her voice abrasive with urgency.

"Why? The baby isn't due for months. He'll still be home in time for the birth," Rosa said, confused.

Theresa sighed, frustration boiling under her skin.

"He needs to come home now and be here for Paige. We found out the baby is sick. There's something wrong with her kidneys. We don't know how bad it is yet, but it's consumed Paige. She's not coping. She needs support. She needs him," Theresa pressed.

Rosa nodded, clearly rattled. Without another word, she pulled out her phone and dialled Elliot's number, pressing it to her ear as Theresa stood by, every nerve on edge.

"Elio? Yes, I'm fine. Listen, I need you to come home. It's about Paige-"

Rosa turned to Theresa mid-sentence, her face slack with shock. Slowly she pulled the phone from her ear and let out a heavy sigh.

"He hung up."

CHAPTER ELEVEN

Dear little love,

I had to buy a new concealer today. The dark circles under my eyes are getting harder to hide, and people are starting to notice. I tell them I'm just tired and they make a joke about pregnancy being exhausting.

I don't even have the energy to smile anymore.

I love you.

Mumma

*P*aige laughed, letting the hanger slip through her fingers as she gave up the pretence of browsing. Grace was still going on about the horror story she'd just read online.

"I'm serious," Grace said, shuddering dramatically. "A baby - born with teeth. Ewww, it gives me the heebie-jeebies just thinking about it."

"How does that even happen?" Paige asked, wrinkling her nose.

"No idea, but I knew that kid would come out ugly." Grace shrugged, tossing another onesie into her basket.

"Grace!" Paige gasped.

"What? It's true. Unlike our baby, who will be peak perfection."

Paige's heart melted at that. For weeks, the word 'baby' had carried connotations of fear and illness, of negativity and despair. Hearing Grace talk lovingly about her niece, describing her as 'our baby' and 'perfection' despite her medical condition, infused her with warmth and hope, two things she hadn't felt in months. Her daughter might not have an active father in her life, but she'd be surrounded by family and never lack for love.

"Okay," Paige said, smirking, "but if it's our baby, does that mean you're paying for all those clothes?"

Grace flashed a mock-serious look in Paige's direction. "Oh no, dear sister. I would never dream of robbing you of the joy of spending your money." She finished the sentence with an appalling British accent that made Paige laugh out loud.

They checked out and stepped into the street. The cool spring breeze stung them, the wind biting through their coats as they linked arms together.

"You mock me for being hungry," Grace said, "but shouldn't you be the one nagging me for food?"

Paige's stomach turned…again. She couldn't remember the last proper meal she'd eaten. Snacks, sure - a biscuit here, a piece of fruit there - but nothing filling; nothing nutritious. Food made her nauseous these days, so it was easier to sip coffee and pretend she was fine than admit she was running on fumes.

Grace nudged her shoulder, pointed to a flickering neon sign above a shop doorway. $20 Tarot Readings.

"You've got to be kidding," Paige scoffed.

"Come on! It'll be fun. Something random to top off the day. You've never had one, right?"

"No, because it's a crock."

Grace clasped her hands in mock prayer. "Maybe they'll tell us the baby's gender, then we can find out if they're really legit."

"They have a fifty–fifty shot," Paige muttered.

"Please?" Grace widened her eyes into puppy-dog mode.

Paige sighed, smiling at her sister's antics. "Fine. Lead the way."

They pushed through the painted green door, greeted by wafts of incense and a wash of strange music; upbeat and eclectic; haunting and complex. Brightly coloured Persian-style rugs were layered over each other with no rhyme or reason. At least two dozen lamps were scattered around haphazardly, casting a warm, inviting glow and contributing to the cosy ambience. In the centre of the room, sitting an old wooden table, was a woman dressed head to toe in black.

"Welcome, girls," she said smoothly. "I've been expecting you."

Paige and Grace exchanged a look. Paige was uneasy, while her younger sister practically buzzed with excitement.

"My name is Willow," the woman continued, gesturing to the mismatched chairs across from her. "I know what brings you here and I know the question you wish to ask."

Her gaze landed on Paige and her polished smile softened, replaced with a tinge of sadness. She reached across the table and clasped Paige's hands in her cool, ring-laden fingers.

"You are hurting, child. Grieving what should have been. You believe you played a part in it, but listen to me… there is a snake in the grass. Someone wearing a mask, deceiving everyone but you. That is why you are dangerous to them. You see through their lies."

Paige flinched, Shaun's face forced its way into her mind.

Willow inched back slowly, holding Paige's gaze as she handed her a battered deck of cards. "Shuffle. Hold your question in your heart."

Paige slid the cards between her fingers, willing her doubts and fears into them before passing them back. Grace watched wide-eyed as Willow closed her eyes, breathed deeply, and began to lay the cards out in a cross.

"This is the present," she said, tapping the first. "The Two of Swords. You are at a standstill, but the blindfold is slipping. A choice is coming."

The second card crossed the first. "The obstacle. The Seven of Swords. Deception. A thief in the dark."

Paige's stomach was in knots.

"The foundation," Willow continued, laying a card at the base. "The Moon. Shadows. Intuition. You know more than you admit, even to yourself."

To the left, another card. "The past. The Three of Swords. Betrayal. Heartbreak. But the storm is clearing."

Finally, the top card. "The near future. The Tower. What was built on lies will fall. Painful, yes. But necessary."

Paige let out a shaky breath. "So… things get worse?"

"For a time," Willow's tone was measured, "but only to clear the way for what's real."

She tapped the last card, set just outside the cross. "The advice. The Star. Hope. Healing. A reminder that this story begins and ends with you. Not with them."

Paige's throat burned as she swallowed hard. Her fingers itched to touch the card, to believe it.

"The choice is yours," Willow explained, "it always has been."

By the time Paige arrived home, the tarot reader's prophetic words weighed heavily on her mind. Looking around her apartment, she was struck by its chaos and disorder - dirty dishes stacked on the counter, unopened mail strewn across the table, laundry spilling from a basket. When did this happen? How did her lovely home, her sanctuary, descend into this god-awful mess?

Paige stood rooted to the spot, toes flexing in her tight leather boots. The weight of her reality - the untidy apartment, her impending responsibilities, her own fractured heart - pinned her in place, trapped, unable to move forward; today's shared laughter with Grace a brief reprieve from her shadowed memories.

As she had done so many times before, Paige forced her feet to move, past the dishes, the laundry, the detritus that was her life. She reached her bedroom, stripped down mechanically, and slid beneath the sheets, the bed no longer her safe haven.

In the stillness, she let her eyes adjust to the velvet darkness before finding the patch of discoloured paint in the corner of the ceiling that represented one of the few constants in her life these days. Eyes transfixed, she let her mind wander, replaying every choice, every word, every mistake that had brought her here. Alone. Waiting.

CHAPTER TWELVE

Dear little love,

I saw a woman in a shop window today who looked so worn and haggard. I looked at her eyes, struck by her haunted expression. It took me a long time to realise it was my own reflection.

What is happening to me? I feel like I am slowly disappearing into nothingness. I don't know how to stop it.

Love,

Mumma

Elliot

Elliot slammed his phone down on the bar, the heavy thud drawing a few glances his way. He let out a loud huff of frustration, his chest heaving. How dare his mother bring up the one person who had caused him so much pain?

Grabbing the crystal glass in front of him, he threw his head back, letting the amber liquid scorch its way down his throat. It set his insides ablaze, exactly the burn he was craving. His head began to swim as he turned to the man beside him.

"What did she want?" Shaun asked casually, sipping his own drink.

"She wanted me to come home. Apparently, Paige needs me," Elliot sighed, the words acrid on his tongue. No matter how much he drank, no matter how many strangers he slept with or how much money he gambled away, the ache in his chest refused to leave. The longing for her.

Shaun scoffed beside him and waved at the bartender to pour another round.

Vegas had been Shaun's idea. Convincing his friend to tell his mother he had a new movie to film had been too easy. Elliot trusted him blindly and Shaun relished the hold he had over him. He was the puppeteer; Elliot his marionette, powerless to fight the invisible strings that manipulated him.

For years, Shaun had lived in Elliot's shadow. They had met on the set of their first TV show. Ironically, Shaun had been cast as the lead, Elliot a minor recurring character. In the years since, Shaun had scraped and fought for every miserable role while his buddy skyrocketed to fame. He loathed it. Deep down, Shaun quite liked

Elliot, but watching his rival's life unravel before his eyes thrilled him even more.

Shaun shoved the refilled glass closer to him. "Go on," he urged.

Elliot didn't hesitate. He grabbed the glass and threw it back, chasing the fleeting hope that maybe this shot would be the one to finally dull the pain.

For a while, he'd been racked with guilt, convinced he'd single-handedly destroyed their relationship. Thanks to Shaun, he could finally see it wasn't only his cross to bear. Paige had had a hand in blowing it up too.

With every passing day, his grief curdled into resentment. When they had first arrived in Las Vegas, his mind went straight to their last Christmas - the one where she had given him the poker set - a custom mahogany box engraved with their initials, lined with silk, loaded with personalised cards and chips. During one of their early dates, he had reminisced about playing poker with his aunts when he was a boy. In true Paige style she had stored this tidbit in her brain until the time was right, bringing this memory back to life with her thoughtful gift.

When he unwrapped it, he felt a rush of love so fierce it almost knocked him off his feet. He could still see himself pulling out a chip, turning it between his fingers, watching his reflection in the gold inlay.

That Christmas, they'd revisited a question they'd danced around for years: *How about we elope to Vegas?* They'd laughed about hiring an Elvis impersonator and a gaudy 24-hour chapel; about him in a tux and sneakers, Paige in a vintage mini dress. Kissing under a Vegas sign, riding off in a Cadillac - it had sounded perfect. It sounded like *them*.

But under the dazzling glare of the blinding Vegas lights, he realised that dream was gone. He was living a nightmare.

"Fuck that bitch!" Shaun snickered, signalling for yet another refill. Elliot nodded along, wallowing deeper in his pit of despair.

Paige's lies had almost killed him. Yes, he who was adored by fans worldwide and had more money than he knew what to do with, legitimately believed he was undeserving of Paige's attention or her affection. For this reason, when he sensed her pulling away, absorbed by her latest work, his self doubt took over and the rational part of his brain was replaced by paranoia. It dragged him into the darkness where old wounds fester. So instead of fighting for her, he chose to abandon her first. Do unto others before they do to you.

Downing another drink, his mind circled back to the last time his life made sense - curled up on the lounge next to his love, her hand over his as she guided his touch to the baby growing inside her tummy. How he wished he could go back!

Staring blankly into the distance, Elliot wondered if there was any way to undo the past. Recognising the dangerous glimmer of hope in his friend's glassy eyes, Shaun angled forward, knowing he needed to squash it.

"Can you believe that woman?" he sneered, his voice low and conspiratorial. "Who in their right mind would do that? Get a man to raise another guy's kid without even telling him? You must be seriously fucked in the head to pull something like that."

The perverse pleasure Shaun got from clocking Elliot's distress was immense. But he didn't care. Not one bit.

"I say we find you another woman. Someone hotter than Paige, not that that's hard. Then show her off to the paps. That oughta show her!" Shaun said, grinning wickedly.

For a moment, Elliot, caught in Shaun's deceitful web, actually considered it before common sense kicked in. "No... I can't. I want to keep this out of the public eye. Especially with her new book coming out soon..."

Shaun cut him off sharply, his fury blazing. "Fuck that, man! Fuck her!" he barked louder than he intended, causing heads to turn their way.

Elliot shrank back in embarrassment, but Shaun only smirked, an idea forming behind his cold blue eyes. Leaning toward the bartender, Shaun whispered something inaudible.

The woman hesitated, eyebrows lifting in surprise, but after a beat she winked at him and handed over a bottle from beneath the bar with a knowing smile.

Elliot, too deep in his alcohol-induced haze to register any alarm bells, missed the exchange. He never stood a chance; Shaun's jealousy and thirst for control egging them on. In a matter of hours, the bottle was almost empty and Elliot a slurring wreck, barely able to hold himself upright. Shaun wasn't far behind but, unlike Elliot, his mind was sober and razor sharp. The night was turning out exactly like he had wanted.

The world around Elliot faded to black in fragments.
Heavy breathing.
Black.
Sloppy kisses.
Black.
The cloying smell of roses.
Black.
A ring slipping onto his finger.
Black.
"I do…"
Black.

CHAPTER THIRTEEN

Dear little love,

I lied again today. I told the doctor I'm fine. I said I'm sleeping, eating, coping, living. The usual lies.

I think I've become too good at saying them. I don't even feel guilty anymore. Maybe that's the scary part? Lying feels easier than being honest.

How can I bring you into this mess?

Love,

Mumma

Sunlight streamed through gauzy curtains, tugging Elliot out of a heavy, aching sleep. For a fleeting second, before the world came into focus, he felt the warmth of a body beside him and thought he was home. With Paige.

A lazy sexy smile began to form. His Paige. He rolled over, ready to pull her into his arms. And froze.

A tangle of wiry, over-bleached blonde hair spilled across the pillow. Not Paige. Never Paige.

His stomach dropped. His pulse hammered in his ears. Nausea ripped through him as he bolted upright; his weakened state no match for the punishing force. He barely made it to the bathroom before he collapsed to his knees, retching into the toilet.

This wasn't the first stranger he'd fallen into bed with lately, but it was the first time he'd woken up beside one. Usually, he sent them away before the night was over, before daylight could shine a spotlight on his shame.

His stomach lurched violently. "Could you not?" came a sharp, high-pitched voice from the bed. Bile still burning his throat, he managed to slowly, agonizingly, turn his head towards the owner of the voice, ready to ask her to leave. But what he saw on her left hand made his body revolt once more - a massive pear-shaped diamond, very gaudy and very oversized, catching the sun's morning rays like a cruel joke.

A ring? A wedding ring?

He slumped against the cold tile, sweat slicking his forehead, mind clawing for answers. Surely not! The blonde sauntered into the bathroom completely naked, her surgically sculpted body a parody of perfection. She admired herself in the mirror, smirking at her reflection, before winking at him crumpled on the floor. "Don't you wanna see your wife naked?" she teased.

The word 'wife' detonated in his chest like dynamite. Elliot shook his head, his voice ragged. "What did you just say?"

"I'm your wife, idiot." She leaned against the doorframe, totally unbothered. "Name's Lexus."

He blinked, confusion and contempt darting across his face. "Lexus? Like the car?"

She jutted her chin. "Yeah. And?"

He buried his face in his hands, groaning. "How the hell did this happen?" he rasped.

"You joked about marrying me," she said breezily. "I said I'd only say yes if you bought me a big-ass ring, so you stumbled off to Cartier, waving your credit card like some drunk prince, and dragged me to a chapel." She thrust her hand out, twisting the diamond so shards of light reflected in his eyes.

His stomach flipped violently. "No, no, that didn't happen."

"Oh, it did," she confirmed. "Your friend was there; he gave me the ring box when you dropped it."

The door clicked open behind her.

"Morning, newlyweds!" Shaun's voice was too bright, too smug, as he strolled in with a spare keycard dangling from his fingers.

Elliot's head snapped up, his voice cracking. "What did you do?"

Shaun spread his arms wide, grinning like a man who'd just won the lottery. "What do you mean? I'm just here to celebrate the happiest day of your life, buddy."

Lexus purred, leaning into Shaun as though they were long lost friends. "I was just telling him about last night, Shaun. He could barely stand, but he made it through the vows. Romantic, really."

Elliot's stomach heaved again. "You… you set me up."

Shaun's grin sharpened. "Relax, Prince. Vegas is for fun - you'll thank me later."

"Thank you?" Elliot's voice broke. "You've destroyed me."

Shaun clapped him on the back, laughing like nothing in the world was wrong. "Destroyed? Nah. You just upgraded."

But Elliot knew better. Paige would find out. Some trashy tabloid would run an exclusive and his career, any chance of a reconciliation with Paige and his entire future would be obliterated.

Stagger to the sink, he gripped the porcelain until his knuckles blanched. He stared at the stranger reflected in the bathroom mirror - a pale imitation of the man he used to be.

Paige

Over two thousand miles away, Paige sat motionless on the edge of her bed, trying to make sense of the incomprehensible. Idly scrolling through her phone, a headline had grabbed her attention: *De Luca Finally Finds His 'Happily Ever After' - And It's Better Than Any Book.*

The accompanying photo sucker-punched her, paralysing her mind and body. Elliot, dishevelled in a dirty button-up, was kissing a platinum blonde in a barely-there dress, a huge garish ring on her finger. It only took a few heartbeats before the familiar stirrings of pain replaced the shock. It was merciless, unrelenting.

Paige had been trying to find the motivation to get up and start her day when she came across the photo. Her morning routine had not changed since she first met Elliot - wake up an hour earlier than necessary, take a long shower and sit at the kitchen counter with cereal and a coffee while doomscrolling through social media. It had been her one indulgence before the madness of the day began; her me-time, peaceful and unhurried. It filled her cup enough so she could be everything to everyone else the rest of the day.

Elliot, on the other hand, was wired differently. He had to hit the gym before breakfast every day. At first, he tried to coax her along, insisting she would love the endorphin hit as a daily kickstarter. They both knew that was a lie and, eventually, with good grace, he stopped asking, leaving her to her private time.

Now that Elliot no longer lived at the apartment, she lingered in bed longer and longer, delaying the inevitable - having to face the day alone. Catching up on the day's news from bed gave her some respite before her turbulent emotions took hold, but today, that moment was stolen from her. The fragments of her broken heart had turned into dust. There was no going back now. She was really doing this on her own.

The screen went black as an incoming call took over.

"Hi, Mum…" she croaked, unable to hide the sadness in her voice.

"You saw?" Theresa's voice was heartbreakingly soft.

"Yeah," Paige rasped. "Yeah, I did." Tears spilled faster now.

"I'm so sorry, honey. He's an idiot. I can't believe he's done this. What can I do?"

"Can you… can you come over?" she managed, her voice breaking completely.

"I… I… I…"

The words crumbled as she collapsed into a broken mess, each convulsing sob pushing her deeper into the abyss from where she feared she would never return.

She felt his presence in everything - in the scarf from their first Christmas draped over his chair; in the pile of photos on her bedside table, resting near the new little outfits she had bought for their daughter. Everywhere. Reminders of the man who had broken her again and again and again.

She forced herself up, her body aching from exhaustion and grief. She needed to get out; needed air. She threw the balcony doors open, fingers fumbling with the handle, before staggering outside trying to leave those feelings behind.

A mild spring breeze swept across her skin as she stepped barefoot onto the concrete, the coolness settling against her feet - a quiet reminder rather than a sting. Manhattan hummed beneath her, the faint scent of magnolias drifting up from the street, but none of it reached her fully. Her pulse thundered louder than the city below, drowning out every trace of the season.

She curled her fingers around the iron railing, drawing in a shaky breath. The metal warmed beneath her grip as she leaned on the hard unwavering material, but even that couldn't soothe the ache tightening in her chest.

She leaned forward, looking at the street six floors below. The bustling city she called home, always vibrant and frenetic, was desolate and lifeless; drained of colour and energy. Tall, soulless concrete buildings cast menacing shadows on the footpath. Even the usual cacophony of horns and sirens did not register, a dull hum in its place.

The pain vanished. In its place came a cold, terrifying numbness - the kind that didn't hurt, which scared her more. A fog crept in, thick and heavy, muffling reason. It would be so easy.

And then she felt it. Faint but undeniable, a flutter beneath her ribs. A kick. Her daughter.

Paige belted out a raw, guttural moan which poked through the mess in her mind, allowing much-needed oxygen to enter her brain. She was not alone. She would never be alone again.

Paige gasped, the sound tearing from her chest like a wound reopening. Her mother's voice pierced the haze, soft but steady. "What can I do?"

Paige clung to those words, like a rope. She pushed herself back from the railing, stumbling until her spine met the cool glass of the balcony door. She slid down to the floor, her palms clammy, her whole body shaking as her head began to swim from hyperventilating. But the flutter came again - her daughter, still moving. Still there. Still alive.

And then she heard it. The frantic pounding of footsteps. A voice calling her name, urgent and breaking.

"Paige!"

Theresa burst through the apartment, her hair a mess, her bag slung across her chest. She rushed toward the balcony, her eyes widening in horror as she saw her daughter crumpled on the floor, tears streaming down her face.

"Oh, my baby!" Theresa's voice cracked as she dropped to her knees, gathering Paige into her arms.

Paige collapsed into her mother's chest, clutching at her shirt with desperate hands as she cried with abandon. Theresa rocked her gently, soothing her with her loving words.

"You're okay. I've got you. I've got you."

For the first time in hours, Paige let herself believe she was okay.
Darkness had not swallowed her.
Not tonight.

CHAPTER FOURTEEN

Dear little love,

The apartment feels too quiet tonight. I keep reaching for the remote thinking music will help, but it only seems to make the silence louder.

You wriggle every now and then, and it amazes me how someone I haven't even met yet can ground me more than anyone else ever has.

Some days I feel like I'm unravelling at the edges, but then you press against me and let me know you're there. There for me. Just like I'm there for you.

We're going to make a great little team!

Love,

Mumma

The smell of disinfectant was strong.

With each breath, Paige felt the heaviness of the last few hours slowly lift.

Her mother had found her on the balcony in a fragile, agitated state. Her momentary loss of control could have had serious repercussions, not just for her, but for her baby and her family too. This awareness broke her heart.

She lay on the hospital bed, the stiff gown irritating the bare skin of her bump, and stared at the monitor to which she was connected. The rhythmic waves of her daughter's heartbeat rolled across the screen, a soothing balm to the racing thoughts in her head.

As she rested her eyes, her mind drifted. To him. The man who had helped create her daughter. The medication she had been given to steady her frayed nerves began to take effect. Reassured that the tablets would not harm her baby, she relaxed enough to allow it to take hold. Little by little, the shaking left her body - the storm had passed. The sound of a chair scraping across the floor pulled her back to the room. She blinked, disoriented, her vision fuzzy from the medication.

When the blur became clearer, she realised she was staring at her brother, Jasper. He looked… different. His normally polished appearance was gone; his cheeks flushed, eyes red and swollen, hair a mess. Usually well put-together, the young man now looked like a shell of his former self.

He sniffed, wiped at his nose and opened his mouth to speak, only to stop himself. Instead, he just looked at her; looked at her with such pain. And guilt.

Paige lifted her hand to reach for his, but her drugged coordination failed her. Jasper, already knowing what she needed, reached out and caught her hand before it fell. Without a word, he threaded his fingers through hers and began tracing slow, steady circles on her skin.

His fingers were rough, like sandpaper, toughened with calluses that spoke of years spent working with his hands. The contrast struck her immediately - her own hands were soft, pens and keyboards her tools of trade to bring her stories and dreams to life. Her sibling's hands by comparison were meant for building, for crafting someone else's vision into something tangible.

She created worlds on paper. He created them in wood and stone.

There were things she wanted to say; things she needed to say, but once again, the words escaped her. This was becoming a pattern. Stealing a breath, she opened her mouth to see what would come out. Before she could say anything, he jumped in, unable to lift his eyes from their hands. "Why?" he croaked.

"I... I don't know," she replied, shame heavy in her voice.

"Why are we here?" His voice cracked slightly, but his grip on her hand tightened.

Paige blinked at him, stunned by the question. It wasn't at all what she'd expected.

"Where?"

"Here. Why are you in this bed? Why are you still mourning the death of that toxic relationship? Why are you letting this man dictate how you feel about yourself?" His voice grew louder, the anger and resentment thick in the air.

"I..." Paige opened her mouth to defend herself, but no words came. She turned her head toward the ceiling. The burn in her eyes, her constant companion these last few months, rose again, but this time she didn't fight it.

"Paige," he said more gently, "you are so much stronger than this. This isn't you. I know hormones make things crazy..."

He regretted the words as soon as they left his mouth.

Paige snapped her head toward him, her tears transforming into fury.

"Hormones? You think my not moving on is hormones? You think me being upset about the end of a relationship I invested so much of myself into for three years is just hormones?"

"That's not what I meant and you know it."

Jasper tried to keep his frustration in check, to hide the anger he felt towards his sister. A part of him knew it wasn't her fault, but his concern propelled him onwards.

"Then what did you mean, Jasper?"she challenged.

"I just… I don't know." Scratching at the short stubble on his chin, he tried to make sense of his thoughts.

Paige's voice cracked as she cut in, her words coming faster now, full of emotion.

"I'm trying to figure this out just as much as you are. My life has gone to shit, Jasper. One minute I had it all - not in some gross, clichéd way. I just… I had a clear understanding of what tomorrow would bring. I thought I had a future; a life together with this man, until suddenly, I didn't." Her chest heaved with the effort of her words, Jasper watching her close as she began to unravel.

"Now what? I'm just supposed to keep getting up even though a pretty damn big part of that routine, that life, is gone. I'm just supposed to shrug it off and accept that this is my new normal? How? No, seriously Jasper, how? Tell me how to do it and I'll do it because I would give anything to wake up from this bullshit nightmare."

"P… I…" Jasper stumbled.

"No. You don't get to say my hormones are making me crazy when there is a clear reason why this is happening, and it's not because I'm pregnant."

Jasper exhaled a long breath, his shoulders sagging as he ran a hand through his hair.

"Look, I know you have every right to feel the way you do. You do. God, you do. I just…" He trailed off, shaking his head, his jaw pulsating.

"I don't know what to say anymore, P. Watching you like this - it's killing me too. I guess I just don't know how to help you without saying something wrong. So yeah… I said it wrong. And I'm sorry for that."

His eyes lifted to hers, his voice easing. "I just… I wish you could see what I see when I look at you. You're stronger than this, stronger than him. I hate that he still has this hold over you."

The words hurt, but they were necessary. She now understood the toll this break-up with Elliot had had on them all - herself and her family.

Elliot

On the other side of the country, Elliot kept his eyes on the floor as his wife twirled in front of the mirror, tossing aside outfit after outfit in favour of something shorter, tighter, louder.

He forced himself to appear interested, but the gravity of his drunken error crushed him.

They'd spent the day talking, trying to get to know each other, but all Elliot had learned was that Lexus was an exotic dancer who had been married before. Just how many times before, he was uncertain.

But that wasn't what bothered him. What truly ate at him was how self absorbed she seemed. Her only real question to him was how would she get access to his bank account. As much as he loathed the situation, he couldn't help shake the feeling that this was what he deserved - a punishment for all the pain he had caused Paige.

His mind drifted as Lexus prattled on about her new life in New York. He pictured Paige standing in the middle of what would have been their nursery, barefoot and determined, one hand on her hip as she argued about paint colours. She'd be adamant that it needed to be something soft and calming, like sage or cream, while he'd throw in wild suggestions just to make her roll her eyes.

Woodland creatures, gender-neutral palettes, pastel rainbows - they'd go back and forth for hours, laughing and trading Pinterest screenshots. He could almost hear her voice, light and teasing, as she tossed a pillow at his head for suggesting something nonsensical and outrageous, just to elicit a reaction from her.

He imagined sitting beside her on the floor, Allen key in one hand, while she handed him screws and snacks in equal measure as he clumsily built a cot. Her laughter, soft and tired. The smell of paint lingering in the air.

He longed to be there. To press his palms against her belly and feel the baby move beneath his touch; to fall asleep to the sound of her reading baby name lists aloud, just to see which ones made him groan and her smile. He wanted the late-night runs for ice cream, the tiny kicks at 3am. He wanted the life they'd planned.

He wanted her. He wanted them.

Instead he sat in a hotel room with a woman he did not know, a woman who had taken advantage of his drunken state to marry him for his money, while the love of his life, carrying what he was convinced was another man's child, moved on with hers. Yet somehow, the ache in his chest only grew.

"Are you even listening to me?" Lexus's shrill voice broke through the fog of Elliot's thoughts, sending a shiver down his spine.

"Sorry… yeah. You were saying?" he replied, forcing himself to meet her gaze, silently begging to feel something for the woman in front of him. Anything.

But nothing came.

"I said I'm not living with your mother," she huffed, dramatically tossing a skimpy dress into her suitcase. "We need to find our own place before we move back. On the Upper East Side. Preferably with views of Central Park. I'm not living in Brooklyn like some basic bitch. Oh, and the building has to have at least ten stories. I want views."

She kept talking, issuing a long laundry list of demands, but her new husband had stopped listening. Sitting on the edge of the lumpy hotel bed, he realised the anger he'd once felt, the devastation of being told the baby wasn't his, had dulled, fading into something quieter; something that hurt more. Love. Regret. For Paige.

At the same time, it dawned on him that that chapter of his life was over. He'd already destroyed one relationship. He wouldn't destroy this one too. He refused to have a failed marriage. Even if it killed him.

CHAPTER FIFTEEN

Dear little love,

I feel like guilt is my frequent companion these days. It lives rent-free in my head.

I feel ashamed about everything, even when I know I am blameless. How much I miss him, how much I hate him and for wishing he could feel even a fraction of my pain.

I tell myself good people don't think like that, but the thoughts still come. What kind of an example am I setting you?

Sometimes I think I'm failing you before you even arrive. I'm trying to be better. I promise you.

Love,

Mumma

Paige

"So, Paige... how have you been doing?"

Dr Baker's voice was mild, but the concern in his eyes was impossible to miss. She sat opposite him in his office, wary, awaiting the results of her latest scan.

"I'm fine, thank you," she replied, her voice composed, offering little else. She didn't want to go into detail about the hospital; about what happened that night on the balcony. Nor did she want to explain her new living situation.

After her hospital stint, Paige had moved back in with her mother, swapping the isolation of her lonely apartment for the safety net of her family's love. Her brother and sister had packed up her essential belongings, placing the rest in storage. Just as it had during her younger years, her childhood bedroom became her refuge again - reborn with a fresh coat of paint, inviting new linen and the tiny bassinet that she and her siblings had all slept in, retrieved from the attic.

Dr Baker studied her quietly. The notes he had received from the hospital painted a grim picture:

Acute grief response. Passive suicidal ideation. Difficulty articulating hope for the future. Emotionally fragile. High risk for perinatal complications. Requires close monitoring.

Pleasingly, the woman who sat before him now looked nothing like that; not at all like the woman who had first presented to him all those weeks ago. She was upright and alert, with clear, determined eyes and glowing hair and skin that radiated good health. She softly massaged her bump as she spoke, using the power of touch to communicate with her child. It wasn't just maternal instinct, it was something fierce and instinctively protective - an unbreakable connection of love.

"I want you to know you can tell me anything, Paige," he said, sincerity evident in every word. "Not just as your doctor, but maybe as a new friend."

She looked down at her belly, drawing slow, absent-minded circles across the stretched fabric of her shirt. Her fingers stilled for a beat, then resumed - slower, more intentional.

A hint of a smile tugged at her lips as she looked back up at him.

"I know you know," she said.

His expression shifted, but it was more than sympathy. It was something more powerful. An unspoken understanding settled between them like a weight they both recognised.

"I do," he murmured, his voice lower. The words trailed off, unsure how much of the truth he was allowed to say out loud.

"It's okay," she said, saving him from the silence. "I get it. It's not easy to talk about."

He nodded slowly, as though grateful she'd said it first. "It's not," he admitted. "However, if you ever want to talk about what happened - talk about anything, medical or not - I'm here."

Paige held his gaze, studying him freely. He was so kind and open. Genuine. The brilliant white fluorescent lighting bounced off his hair, the soft grey flecks quiet streaks of wisdom in a sea of black. There was something comforting about it. Trustworthy.

"Thank you," she said softly. And then, with a breath that felt lighter than the ones before, she moved the conversation on to her baby..

"So how is my daughter doing?"

Dr Baker paused, his expression blank, but she knew something was amiss.

"Unfortunately, it's not good news. Her kidneys are continuing to increase in size, and the dilation in the left one is more severe than the right. It's not at a critical level yet, but I think we need to start discussing the option of induction.

"I'm hoping we can hold out until 37 weeks, but you're at 28 now, and realistically, I doubt you'll make it to 34. I'm sorry."

Paige nodded slowly, trying to quell the rising fear bubbling in her stomach and spreading like wildfire throughout her body. Mustering all her strength, she closed her eyes and concentrated on her breathing - slowly, in and out, in and out - until the calm started to return.

It'll be okay. We'll be okay. We can do this together.

Basic and simple. This had been her mantra since the night she left the hospital. For some reason she could not understand, the repetition would bring her back to the present when her emotions began to unravel. When nights stretched on and on and sleep eluded her, the chant worked like a powerful sedative, settling her and rocking her to rest.

This time, though, something was different. The world slowed and she opened her eyes wide, finally aware that a thumb - a male's thumb - was rhythmically stroking the back of her hand.

Dr Baker was beside her; when he had moved from his desk she had no idea. His hand rested over hers, his thumb gently massaging her skin, grounding her more than any breathing exercise or coping strategy ever had.

His voice reached her next. Low, steady, unwavering. He told her she was safe; that the baby was safe; that everything was going to be alright.

Trying to make sense of the moment, Paige looked up and met his eyes. Something warm fluttered inside her chest - both confusing and comforting. Not desire. Not entirely. Just… relief. A simple moment where her body stopped shaking and the world stopped spinning. She didn't question it, she didn't have the energy. Paige had always known he was handsome, but the way he looked at her - gentle, steady and free of judgement - slipped past her defences or at least what remained of them. He didn't rush her; didn't shame her. He spoke to her like a human, one who was wounded but not broken beyond repair. Paige felt that tug in her chest that told her she was starved of this feeling.

Maybe she had felt it in earlier appointments and been too shattered and caught up with what was happening with Elliot to notice. Maybe she blamed it on hormones or exhaustion. Now, sitting here in his quiet office, she finally recognised it for what it was: the feeling of being safe.

She didn't think of boundaries.

Or lines.

Or the fact that he was too close.

It didn't occur to her that this could be wrong.

She held his gaze a moment too long. He didn't look away. And that stillness - quiet, steady, almost tender - felt like something precious.

Later she would understand; would see the line.

But not now, not here. Not with him looking at her like that.

THREE QUICK KNOCKS STARTLED THEM, fracturing the moment. The spell broken, Dr Baker cleared his throat and slowly, almost reluctantly, withdrew his hand. He stood and turned towards the door expectantly, trying to ignore the air charged with unspoken desire.

"Come in," he instructed, his professional mask back in place, erasing the memory of what had occurred just as quickly as it happened.

Paige adjusted her jacket, the imprint of his thumb on her skin still tingling. She wasn't sure what any of it meant, but she knew one thing: she wanted to find out.

"Sorry to bother you, Dr Baker," the receptionist said. "Beatrice has dropped Harriet off and left. What should I do?"

Dr Baker let out a big sigh and squared his shoulders back. Paige scrutinised him carefully, trying to decipher how he felt about this interruption. He wasn't irritated, Paige concluded, just frustrated; like another responsibility had been added to an already full day. Odd really.

"It's okay, Janet. I'll handle it."

From behind the hem of her skirt, a small girl peeked out. Four or five years old. Dark braids. Wide eyes. A worn teddy bear tucked under her chin like a shield.

Paige watched quietly, curiosity blooming. Who was she? Why had she been left here?

"Darling," he said gently, crouching to the girl's level. "Can you go with Janet while I finish up?"

The little girl nodded, put her thumb in her mouth and followed Janet, silent as a shadow.

He turned back to Paige, rubbing the bridge of his nose.

"Sorry."

"You don't have to apologise," she said. "I should let you get back to… all of that."

He nodded but didn't move.

"Paige? I meant what I said," he told her. "You can talk to me and not just as your doctor. What you're going through is a lot. You and your daughter deserve support. Not just clinical support - real support."

His voice was steady. Honest. No trace of performance.

Appreciating his candour, she gave a nod and a heartfelt smile. As she gathered her things and moved towards the door, he blocked her path. Reaching into his pocket he removed a small piece of paper, edges bent.

"Please," he carefully said, holding it out. "If you need anything, call me. It's my personal number."

There was a pause - one that seemed to stretch longer than necessary - but he persisted. Exchanging quick goodbyes, she took it and left, leaving him alone in the silence of his office.

Liam sat back in his chair, staring into nothingness, lost in his swirl of thoughts. This was becoming a pattern.

Everyone who knew him could tell you that Liam was a caring and present doctor; one who prioritised his patients and their wellbeing. If he had a fault, it was that occasionally he carried their worries too close, compassion blurring the lines he was meant to hold. Yet he had never once crossed a professional boundary, always managing to negotiate that fine line with his integrity intact. Until now.

There was something about Paige; something that touched his soul. He'd felt that the first time he met her, every subsequent visit reinforcing the fact. He didn't usually lie awake at night hoping someone would reach out to him. He never panicked when someone's breathing quickened after receiving bad news, however when she had spiralled into that panic attack, he hadn't thought clinically or logically. He had just felt a singular, urgent need to protect her. Help her. Save her.

He rubbed the hint of stubble on his face, trying to clear the confusion in his mind. This wasn't part of the job, but it was too late for that, wasn't it? He took one last deep breath, stood up and straightened his coat. A scared little girl was in the waiting room, and she needed him now.

It had been a quiet dinner, the kind where conversation was limited to polite murmurs and clinking cutlery. Pleasantries were swapped, but nothing of note was said.

Paige sat at the end of the table, pushing peas around her plate long after she'd finished eating. Across from her, her mum collected dishes one by one, offering Paige a loving smile as she reached for hers. Paige managed a weak one in return.

Her mum looked tired, the kind of tired that settles into one's bones making you look and feel older than you really are. Worn down and weathered. Watching her shuffle to the kitchen, Paige felt a tug at her heart. As much as she wished it weren't true, she knew she was the cause of most of her mother's anguish.

She hadn't needed much convincing to move back into the family home after the balcony incident. Starved of a safe cocoon, the idea of being surrounded by loved ones and the comfort of the familiar, was impossible to resist. She was ashamed to admit she hadn't thought twice about how everything would impact on her dear mother. Or her stepfather.

Lou was standing by the sink, rinsing his plate. Smiling, he caught Paige looking at him. He was a big muscular man - tall and broad. Due to his stature, he took up a lot of physical space and his presence was felt everywhere. Everyone in the neighbourhood called him Bruiser. Rumour had it that he knocked a guy out in the Costco car park once after a run-in over a park, though her mother insisted it came from all the time he spent boxing as a teen. Regardless, the nickname amused his family greatly because he would do anything - absolutely anything - to avoid confrontation. Let's face it, if you looked up 'gentle giant' in the dictionary, you'd see his picture.

"How are you doing, kid?" he asked, quiet but firmly.

"I'm fine," Paige responded automatically.

He raised an eyebrow, a flicker of amusement behind the concern. "You're lying to me."

"No, I'm not," she replied, a little too quickly.

He shook his head, stepping away from the sink and folding the towel over his shoulder. "I've known you a long time now. I watched you grow from that shy teenager who wouldn't look anyone in the eye into the semi-capable adult who moved out before she was ready." His lips quivered slightly, but his voice remained even. "I know how to read you, Paige, and you're wearing thin."

Paige looked down at her hands, picking at a chipped nail. "I don't know what you mean," she murmured, feigning ignorance.

But she knew exactly what he meant. She didn't want to talk about how, in a fleeting, desperate moment, she'd wondered if anyone would miss her if she weren't around. She still felt the sting of that shame and grief, clinging to her like smoke, and while she wanted to be honest about her feelings, she also wanted to spare him the worry.

He crossed the room slowly, his worn boots soft against the linoleum, and pulled out the chair next to hers. He didn't sit right away, just rested a hand lightly on her shoulder and crouched so they were eye level.

"I know you're hurting," he said. "I know you feel lost; like the ground beneath your feet keeps shifting and you don't know which way is up anymore. I just need to tell you something, kid. I'm here and I'd do anything for you - not just as your mum's husband, but as your dad. And I'll do the same for your daughter, too."

Tears welled up in her eyes.

"It's okay to feel broken; to not know what to do. But if you ever feel like you can't stand up anymore, you tell me and I'll help you stand. I'll hold you up as long as you need."

The love and sincerity in those words hit Paige like a freight train. The tears started to flow and there was nothing she could do to stop them. Not trusting herself to speak, she just sat there, clutching her hands in her lap, letting him see what she couldn't say.

He tucked a loose strand of hair behind her ear before continuing "You scared me, kid," he murmured, voice cracking now.

"Losing you is one of the worst things I could imagine. You may not be my blood, but you are my daughter."

Paige opened her mouth to respond, but no words came out. With wet cheeks, she reached out to Lou and he pulled into a tight bear hug, clasping her to his chest like he would never let her go.

For the first time in a long while, she felt at peace.

CHAPTER SIXTEEN

Dear little love,

I'm not a religious person by nature, but today I prayed.

I prayed to any and all the gods, whoever might be listening, for your kidneys to heal themselves.

My greatest wish is that I'll wake up one day and find this was all a bad dream. Until then, I'll continue with these prayers - inviting hope in. Who knows, it may find us!

Little one, rest assured that while I am not very brave myself, I am finding inner reserves of strength - strength I never knew I had - which is making me be brave for you.

For you, I can do anything.

Love,

Mumma

. . .

Elliot

lliot sat slumped in the back of the Uber, his gaze fixed on the rain slicked window. The car was winding its way through the streets towards the apartment he would now share with a woman he didn't love and maybe never could. An apartment, never a home.

His stomach twisted with unease, a queasy reminder of the mess he'd made of everything.

He glanced at Lexus, who sat beside him, her face pressed to the glass like an excited child on a school excursion.

"Isn't this so exciting?" she cooed.

"Yeah…" Elliot's voice was hollow, devoid of expression.

It's not that he disliked Lexus or harboured any resentment towards her. He was just indifferent, uninterested. She was nothing to him.

She wasn't Paige.

And that truth was eating him alive.

Vivid memories of Paige assailed him from every direction, crashing into him mercilessly. He could smell the faint mix of vanilla and her natural scent on her soft alabaster skin; the way his heart skipped a beat whenever he heard her light, unguarded laugh. He could see the way she'd glance at him from across a room, talking to others while shyly keeping tabs on his movements; remember lying beside her at night, feeling her warmth seeping into every part of him and believing he'd finally found where he belonged. With her. She *was* home.

Not any more. He'd burnt his home to the ground with his own hands. The scent, the laughter, the smiles - all of it - belonged to another lifetime. To a better man.

Where had it all gone so wrong?

The answer clawed at the back of his mind. His manager's warnings, the tabloids, the pressure to "clean up his image." After the breakup with Paige had become public knowledge, Lexus had looked conveniently beautiful, polished and drama-free on the surface. She'd said the right things in the interviews he had been forced to participate in. She knew how to play the game. For a moment, Elliot had convinced himself that was enough.

"So when do I get my credit card?" Lexus asked abruptly.

"Huh? What credit card?"

"Well, we're married now. Obviously we're going to have joint bank accounts so, you know… cards, spending limits, perks. I'll need access if I'm your wife, right?"

Elliot blinked at her, the words slow to register. For weeks he'd been drowning in heartbreak, gnawing guilt and the crushing truth that he'd destroyed the only thing that had ever meant anything to him. Somewhere in the wreckage, he'd landed here, with a woman who cared more about what she could get from the relationship than the relationship itself.

Before he could form a reply, the Uber rolled to a stop outside their new building.

"Home sweet home," Lexus said, sliding out with her Prada bag slung over her shoulder.

Elliot followed slowly, dragging his feet. Every step felt heavier than the last because he was stuck in limbo, caught in no man's land between his past and his present.

The building was everything Lexus had asked for, and quite frankly, Elliot was impressed. Perfect neighbourhood, above ten floors and, although she hadn't specified it, he knew for a fact a few of his celebrity peers lived in the same complex.

He glanced at his new bride and reached for her hand. Instead of anything resembling warmth and affection, he felt cold, unyielding skin. She yanked her hand away.

"Don't," she snapped. "You'll ruin the manicure you paid for."

Elliot swallowed his embarrassment as they stepped into the building's classically inspired, heritage lobby. Refusing to acknowledge the door man, Lexus took in the majestic high ceilings with gorgeous crown mouldings, silk wallpaper and antique furnishings with a grimace, her nose scrunching in disapproval.

"This is… retro," she muttered, forcing a thin smile.

Not what she wanted, not even close.

As they entered the apartment with its own private elevator, Elliot couldn't help but feel proud. The place was stunning - a large, open plan space with floor to ceiling windows that offered a panoramic view of Central Park in all its glory. His assistant had worked miracles furnishing it on such short notice.

But the moment was short-lived.

"Seriously? This is it?" Lexus gawked, her face twisted in disbelief.

Elliot blinked, stunned.

"You don't like it?"

"No. It's horrible. I can't be seen living here."

Her high, razor-edged voice rang through the apartment as she stomped her feet like a child, hands balled into a fist by her side. The sight of a grown woman reacting in this way, criticising a multimillion dollar luxury apartment with what must be some of the best views of the city, floored him. Beneath her tantrum, fleetingly, he witnessed a flicker of panic, quickly replaced with designer indignation.

"This place doesn't say anything about us," she said, softer now, but no less critical. "People are going to think we're… boring. I mean, where is the second floor?"

Elliot's ears burned with humiliation and regret.

""I… I… I'm sorry. I don't know what I can do…" he stammered.

"You can start by finding us a new place. Something that doesn't look like it was designed before electricity was invented." Her piercing voice increased in volume and pitch. "You've really let me down,

Elliot. Badly. Do you even care about me? About this marriage? Or am I another thing you've stopped caring about."

Her words struck him like slaps. Stunned by the evil in her voice, he was unable to move - a deer caught between the headlights. It was as if she'd just caught him in bed with someone else. Before he could say anything - defend himself, apologise, admonish her about her own behaviour or even console her - Lexus lunged at him. Her manicured hand dove into the back pocket of his jeans, yanking out his wallet.

"Lexus? Lexus! LEXUS!"

She ignored him completely. Purposely and methodically, she opened the wallet, removed his cash and credit card, and threw everything else on the floor. Making sure she had his attention, she pirouetted on her six inch heels with dramatic flair and exited the apartment, slamming the door behind her.

Once again, Elliot could not move, struck silent by his wife's outrageous behaviour. When he snapped back to reality, he dropped to the ground and looped his arms around his knees. He couldn't believe his life.

Heartbreak. Humiliation. Regret. Repeat.

He couldn't do this anymore.

He couldn't outrun the hurt.

He needed to talk to Paige.

He needed closure.

CHAPTER SEVENTEEN

Dear little love,

I keep saying sorry, even when no one asks me to apologise. Maybe that's what happens when you start to believe every bad thing is your fault.

People keep telling me I did nothing wrong, but I can't accept that. If I did everything right, everything I was supposed to do, how did I end up here?

Your grandmother says I need to forgive myself first in order to properly heal. She says I need to give myself some grace.

This makes sense logically, but is simplistic in my view. It ignores the fact we are human, and humans are inherently emotionally-driven beings. I'm a living, breathing testament to that.

So what do I do? How do I give myself grace?

I talk to you, little one.

I share my thoughts and my dreams with you in the hope I will one day be able to look back at this time of my life and know I am a strong, resilient woman raising another strong, resilient woman.

From bad comes good.

Love,

Mumma

Paige

Paige tapped her foot, trying to calm her wild thoughts as she waited for good news from her ultrasound.

She shifted uncomfortably on the bed, looking at the hospital gown clinging to the rounded shape of her belly where fresh stretch marks traced delicate lines across her skin - shimmering, tangible reminders of the life growing inside her. She wasn't sure if she wore them with pride yet or if she was still trying to accept the way her body was changing. Time would tell.

She glanced around the room, taking in the large wall featuring dozens and dozens of baby photos - all delivered by Dr Baker. The images were adorable, the cuteness sending her ovaries into over-drive. Some bubs appeared to be smiling (or just had wind), some were pink and tense, their faces screwed up in angry cries; some were as bald as a badger, others had manic mops of hair. All photos were labelled with names.

Paige found herself studying them, hoping for inspiration for her own daughter's name.

There was a picture of a chubby, blonde newborn. Paisley. Paige scrunched up her nose. Definitely not.

There was an Alice. Several Janes. A Carly. Quite a few Destinys spelt more ways than she ever thought possible - Destiny, Destinee, Destineigh, Destynea, Dhestineeh. Lordy! Cleo. Lexus.

Lexus! She scoffed under her breath, shaking her head. Who names their baby after a car, for goodness sake? She smirked at the absurdity of it, unaware in that peaceful moment, just how much she would come to hate that name.

Paige's phone rang from inside her handbag, resting on the chair beside the bed. With a loud sigh, she shifted awkwardly, one hand bracing her lower back as she rolled off the table.

Unknown caller.

She frowned. "Who the hell...?" she muttered, answering anyway.

"Hello?"

She tried to keep her voice nondescript, hoping it wasn't another journalist fishing for gossip about her book tour, about Elliot or about why she'd vanished from the spotlight. No one had figured out she was pregnant yet and she wanted to keep it that way. The last thing she needed was speculation about whether the baby was real, or worse, a publicity stunt.

"Paige..."

Her breath caught. Her chest fluttered - an involuntary response to the devastatingly deep and alluring voice that haunted her dreams. She stiffened. No, she wouldn't be drawn in after all this time.

"What do you want?" she snapped, her tone hardening.

"I just want to talk," Elliot whispered.

"The time for talking is done."

"Please, Paige. I need answers."

She let out a bitter laugh. "You need answers? You left me while I was pregnant to marry someone else! What the hell do you think I owe you?"

His silence cut through the line.

"Please… just once. Meet me. Let me explain. I need closure."

"No," she said firmly, then louder. "No!"

She ended the call with a trembling hand.

A riot of conflicting emotions surged through her simultaneously, knocking her off balance. Her heart thundered and her breath came in short, uneven gasps. The adrenaline that had started coursing through her veins at the very first sound of his voice evaporated, her damp, clammy palms the only evidence Elliot had been in touch.

Before she could fully relegate that incident to her past, a knock sounded at the door.

"Ms Lawson?" came Dr Baker's warm voice just as the door opened.

His joy at seeing her again dissolved as soon as he saw her wide-eyed expression. It was evident something was amiss.

"Are you okay?" he asked, as he crossed the room and placed a steady hand on the small of her back.

Paige flinched at the contact before accepting the implied offer, half-turning to lean into him.

"Yes… no… I don't know." The words were warbled, torn straight from her throat.

"Here, come sit down. Let's just take a second, okay?"

She perched on the edge of the bed, barely noticing that Dr Baker had pulled a stool from the corner of the room and was sitting between her legs. Even his feather light touch on her thighs escaped her.

"Do you want to tell me what happened?" he asked, airily patting her.

"My ex called me."

Those four words stopped him cold, but he didn't let it show. He just kept patting her leg.

"Oh? What did he want?"

"He said he needed to talk. Said he needed answers."

"Answers to what?"

"I don't know," she snapped, finding some loose skin near her cuticles and pulling it sharply. "I don't even know if I care. I don't want to see him. I don't want to talk to him."

He paused, choosing his words carefully. "I understand. Truly. I know this might not be what you want to hear, but maybe it's what you need to hear. Sometimes closure doesn't come from others, it comes from asking the questions you've been too hurt to say out loud."

In the wake of her silence, he knew he shouldn't have said anything. He had overstepped the mark, reacting purely because he could see how hurt she was. God, what was wrong with him? He was her doctor. This wasn't supposed to happen. He thought he'd drawn the line months ago but, every time her name appeared on his schedule, he caught himself counting the hours until he could see her again.

"I don't need answers," she muttered, though the audible ache in her voice seemed to suggest otherwise. "He deserted me; deserted us."

The doctor didn't say anything, just sat and watched as her inner turmoil played out on her face. No translation was needed.

Why did he leave? Why wasn't I enough? Why didn't he love me the way I loved him? Why couldn't he love our baby?

She blinked, her eyes glassy.

Maybe she didn't need answers. Maybe she did just need to be heard.

"Don't do it for you... do it for her."

He didn't push her further. Dr Baker simply reached for the gel and the wand, and Paige, wordlessly, lay back and pulled up her gown, baring her belly like an offering to the gods.

The machine hummed to life. As the wand glided over her skin, the monitor flickered and there she was. Her daughter; tiny limbs flailing like a storm in slow motion, a swirl of life and light on the screen.

The image blurred as Paige was once again overcome by a whirlwind of feeling. Not because of Elliot, nor even because of the call, just the intensity of her love for her child.

Paige settled into the moment and knew he was right. She had promised herself a long time ago that her daughter's needs would always come first. Her baby deserved a father. If there was a chance she could broker a relationship between the two of them, she owed it to her daughter to try.

"Okay..." she acquiesced, the word catching on the lump in her throat.

"You can do this, Paige," he said, smiling that quiet, encouraging smile that somehow always steadied her. "You're an exceptional woman, and your daughter is so lucky to have you."

Something in the doctor's manner drew her eyes from the screen and compelled her to sit up and look at him intently. A spark flashed between them as if someone had lit a match and her heart skipped.

His dark eyes widened, the colour deepening to a deep chocolate brown as he saw his unspoken feelings reciprocated in Paige. Before he could speak, Paige leaned forward and kissed him, consumed by a sudden desire to taste his full lips.

It was soft. Gentle at first.

Dr Baker's hand found the back of her head, fingers threading into her hair as he kissed her back, like he never wanted it to end. Every nerve in her body lit up. Her skin sizzled. Her throat tightened.

And then, just as suddenly, she withdrew, leaving him wanting more.

She stared at him, breathless, her chest rising and falling as the heat slowly gave way to guilt.

"I...I'm so sorry," she stammered, the words rushing out like a confession.

"No... don't be," he murmured, still catching his breath. "That was... wow."

His voice was quiet, awed. She had stolen the air straight from his lungs and he hadn't minded one bit.

"If I go talk to him, will you come with me?"

The words escaped before Paige could stop them. She hadn't planned to ask; hadn't even thought about it until the words had left her mouth. Now that they were out though, she realised how much she needed someone - him - to be there. Not her mother. Not her siblings. Him.

Dr Baker looked taken aback. "Uhh… I don't know, Paige."

"Please," she said quickly. "You don't have to be next to me or anything but, just knowing you're there, I think it might help."

In that moment, the enormity of the last 30 minutes struck her, embarrassment creeping in like a tide. She had received a call from the man who broke her heart and asked her doctor, who was performing an ultrasound on her unborn child, who, by the way, she had also just kissed, to come with her to see the father of her unborn child so she could confront him. It sounded insane. If she included that scenario in one of her books, no one would believe it!

"Forget it," she muttered. "You're right. Stupid idea."

"No. No, it's really not," he said gently. "Just… let me think about it, okay?"

"Yeah… sure."

The shame curled low in her belly, tightening her chest with anxiety. He moved to reset the ultrasound machine and asked if she was ready. She nodded, saying nothing more, trying to collect herself. Lying back down, she tried to swallow the scream in her throat.

What am I even doing?

CHAPTER EIGHTEEN

Dear little love,

I can't believe I lost the bet. It's honestly embarrassing. I bet your Aunt and Uncle that I could name everyone in my high school graduating class. I really thought I had it in the bag. Unfortunately, I didn't, and now they get to choose your middle name.

I'm concerned. They've already been joking about names like Uvula and Poseidon.

Will you ever forgive me?

Love,

Mumma

What does strength really mean?

Is it about physicality or being powerful? Or does it mean having the courage and determination to do something for someone else, even if it rips you apart inside?

The way Theresa saw it, her older daughter was the strongest person she had ever known.

After months of heartache, sleepless nights and private breakdowns, Paige now sat calmly in front of her explaining how she was going to meet the man who had abandoned her. Not for closure. Not even for herself.

For her daughter.

"I know you might not think it's the right thing to do," Paige admitted, "but I have to."

She hoped her mother would disagree; say it was reckless; that she didn't need to do this.

Instead, Theresa nodded.

"I agree with you," she said, her voice level. "Honestly, I'm amazed it's taken him this long to reach out."

Paige blinked, stunned. No argument. No guilt trip.

Before she could respond, Theresa continued, "Where are you meeting him? Do you want me to come with you? Or Lou perhaps? I know he would be more than happy to be an intimidating presence."

"Um… I haven't actually called him back yet. I guess I should do that soon." Paige paused. Without looking up she continued, "And no, you don't need to come… neither does Lou. I already have someone coming with me."

"What? Who?" Theresa asked, narrowing her eyes.

Paige looked directly at her mother, bracing herself for impact.

"Dr Baker's coming with me."

She took a gulp of tea, forgetting to test the temperature first. Pain seared her tongue, making her eyes water.

Theresa stared at her in surprise, trying to make sense of what she was hearing. Streaks of confusion, disbelief and something close to worry caused her to set her mug down so she could ask her daughter an extremely important question:

"Why is your obstetrician going with you to meet your ex?"

Paige shifted in her chair, tracing the rim of her own cup. She wanted to be honest with her mother, so she didn't sugarcoat the truth. "Because I asked him."

"Why in God's name would you do that?" her mother demanded.

Paige hesitated, the question sitting heavily between them. "I don't know exactly," she admitted. "We've had a few… moments. Every time something's happened with Elliot, he's been there. We've gotten closer and then… we kissed."

Her mother's eyes widened so far, Paige thought they might pop right out. "You kissed your doctor?"

"It's not… "

"Don't tell me it's not a big deal," she interrupted. "He's your doctor. He's supposed to be delivering your baby, not delivering emotional drama."

Paige bristled. "We're not dating."

"So what, you're just kissing him for sport? Does that make it better?"

"We haven't slept together, Mum," she shot back.

"Well, that's something, I guess," Theresa said, trying to figure out what had gotten into her child. "Paige, this isn't some rom-com. You're pregnant, you're hurt and you're vulnerable. That's a dangerous combination for making the kind of mistakes that don't just screw you over, they screw over your daughter, too."

The pulse in Paige's jaw throbbed. "It's not like that," she argued.

"Then what is it like?" Theresa's stern gaze took no prisoners. "From where I'm sitting, it looks like you're leaning on a man you barely know because it's easier than standing on your own two feet. You know what happens when you lean too hard on something unstable, don't you?"

Paige swallowed hard, saying nothing.

"It breaks," her mother said quietly. "And when it does, you're the one left on the floor."

Paige could see the concern in her mother's eyes and couldn't blame her. Truth was, she didn't know what she was doing either. It all felt like a mistake she couldn't seem to stop making.

After a long pause, Theresa let out a sigh. "Do you have feelings for him?"

"I don't know." Paige's voice was barely above a whisper. "He just makes me feel… stronger; more confident." She shrugged, the movement small, almost as if she were ashamed of the admission.

"Darling," Theresa said, her voice unyielding, "you are already the strongest person I know. Look at what you've been through! God, you've survived more in the last few months than some people face in a lifetime. Don't bring someone you barely know into this."

Paige swallowed hard. Her mother wasn't wrong. It wasn't fair to drag someone else into her mayhem, especially not someone with his own life, his own responsibilities. With that, a disconcerting thought popped into her head - she didn't even know his first name. To her, he had always just been Dr Baker.

"You're right," she said, feeling herself deflate like a balloon losing air. "I'll call him and tell him not to come."

"That's a good idea." Theresa pressed a kiss against her cheek and left the room, giving Paige space to make the final decision and maybe, to admit to herself that she was falling for someone she barely knew.

Paige lay back on her bed and dialled his number, half hoping he wouldn't answer. After three rings, she heard his greeting. "Hello?"

"Hey… it's Paige. Paige Lawson. Sorry to bother you so late."

"Oh, Paige. It's great to hear from you. Is everything okay?"

That voice. God, it made her dizzy. How could she feel this way about someone she'd only kissed once; someone whose name she didn't even know?

"Yeah, everything's fine. I just… I wanted to talk to you about today."

"Of course," he said gently. "What's on your mind?"

She paused. The words scattered the moment she tried to gather them.

"Paige?" His voice dipped, cautious now. "Are you still there?"

"Yeah. Sorry. I just… I don't really know what to say." She pulled the elastic from her hair and fanned the curls across her pillow, willing herself to say what she needed to say.

"Well, I want to say I really enjoyed that kiss today."

The words stopped her cold. Heat flared up her neck.

"I did too," she admitted softly. "I just... I don't know."

"I imagine you're feeling pretty confused. I know I am," he said. "Is there anything I can do to help? To make things clearer?"

Her voice dropped. Where would she start?

"I just feel like this is...too much. Too many emotions, too fast. You're my doctor - and I barely know you - but when you touch me, it feels like electricity. And my heart...it honestly feels like it might beat out of my chest."

Silence. Again.

"Paige, I feel the same way. I don't want to make this more complicated, but I want to be here for you if I can."

Her heart thudded, fire sparking to life in her chest. She swallowed hard.

"For weeks I've been walking a tightrope trying to stay professional when everything in me wants to cross the line. I'm done pretending," he confessed.

She inhaled sharply.

"I don't think I can be your doctor anymore," he said finally, his voice thick with emotion. "A doctor shouldn't feel this way about a patient. He shouldn't have this overwhelming urge to hold her and kiss her like his life depends on it."

"Then I'll find a new doctor," Paige said, her voice soft but sure. "I just want to get to know you better. I feel like I don't know you at all."

"Well, ask away," he said, a smile audible in his tone. "I'm an open book."

She hesitated, picking at a loose thread in her blanket. "Okay... what's your first name?"

He chuckled low in his throat. "Liam."

"Liam," she repeated, tasting the sound of it. "It suits you."

"Better than Dr Baker?"

"Maybe," she teased, the corner of her mouth lifting.

"What about you?" he asked. "What does Paige Lawson do when she's not making her doctor's life complicated?"

She let out a small laugh, the tension in her chest loosening just a fraction. "Mostly… I write. Read. Drink too much coffee. Argue with my mother about my life choices. You know, the usual."

"I like coffee," he said. "And arguing… maybe not with my mother, but I'm not afraid of a good debate."

She found herself relaxing, toying with the idea of what that might look like - sitting across from him in a coffee shop, leaning in over the table, laughter breaking up the serious moments.

"Favourite food?" she asked.

"Homemade lasagna," he said without hesitation. "But only the way my grandmother used to make it. Every time I try to recreate it, it's just… wrong."

"Mine's sushi," she said. "Although these days, I'd kill for a giant slice of pepperoni pizza."

He laughed. "Pregnancy cravings?"

"Don't judge me, but… sometimes I add a bit of marshmallow fluff on it… for a bit of something else."

"That's not the worst thing I've heard, but I think I can make you a better pizza than that."

She blinked. "You cook?"

"I do a lot of things," he said, voice dropping slightly, almost like a promise.

Her pulse kicked up. God, this was dangerous.

"What about you?" he asked. "Something you've never told anyone."

She went quiet, thinking. "I almost moved to Paris once. I had the ticket and everything, but then Elliot convinced me to stay. He said we'd travel there together one day. We never did."

There was a pause on the line as he digested this confession.

"You still should," he said finally, his voice softer now. "Go to Paris. See the world. Do it for you."

Her throat tightened. "Maybe one day."

Another silence, this one warm and comfortable.

"Paige, I don't know where this is going," Liam continued. I want you to know I'm not here to hurt you. I'm not him. Whatever happens next, I'll never make you feel abandoned."

Her eyes stung, tears falling before she could stop them. "You can't promise that."

"Maybe not," he admitted. "But I can promise I'll try."

She closed her eyes, letting his words settle within her like a stone sinking into deep water.

"Liam?"

"Yeah?"

"Don't make me regret this."

"You have my word."

She laughed awkwardly, not knowing where to take the conversation.

"Where did you go to college?" he asked, shifting gears with a genuine curiosity.

"I didn't, actually. I wrote my first book around the time I sat my SATs, and it just... took off. I never really saw the point after that as I was too busy continuing the series."

She couldn't help the pride that crept into her voice. Her writing was one of the few things in her life that had ever truly been hers.

They talked for hours, voices low, drifting between casual questions and personal truths. From favorite colours to childhood memories, embarrassing stories to quiet insecurities - they left no stone unturned.

"So... you have a daughter?" Paige asked gently, curiosity getting the better of her. It was something they couldn't avoid forever.

"Yeah, I do. Her name's Harriet. She's four." There was a slight pause and then a soft smile in his voice. "She's the smartest little girl I've ever met. And the kindest. She's my everything."

Paige's heart melted.

"That's beautiful. She's lucky to have such an amazing dad."

"I think I'm the lucky one," he said. "She's the most important thing in my life."

"I hope this isn't too nosy, but... what about her mum?"

He sighed, his mood dropping. "Oh, Beatrice. Well, how do I put this nicely? She's not the most hands-on mother."

Paige's chest ached at the thought. How could any mother not want to spend every waking moment with their child?

"I'm sorry," she said sincerely.

"It's okay," he replied. "It means I get Harriet to myself most of the time. She's the light of my life. I don't know what I'd do without her."

"I love hearing how you talk about her. It's seriously beautiful"

Their first proper conversation drifted on the way only the best conversations do - gentle, slow burning, full of shared revelations. Paige sat curled on her bed, watching the first light of dawn streak across the sky.

"It's almost time to get up," Liam said with a sleepy laugh.

"Yeah," she said, reluctantly. "I guess I should let you go. I've loved talking to you."

"I've got to get Harriet ready for preschool."

"Right." She hesitated, heart twisting. "So I guess I'll see you later?"

"Definitely. Maybe lunch?"

She paused. "I was going to call Elliot today. Maybe meet him?"

The undercurrent in her tone changed, a fact not lost on Liam. He understood what she wasn't saying, interpreting what was left unsaid: She didn't want to go, but she would, and she would go alone - not for herself, but for her daughter.

"Okay," he said softly. "Let me know how it goes."

They said their goodbyes, and the call ended, leaving her alone with the one thing she had been avoiding all night.

It was time to call Elliot.

CHAPTER NINETEEN

Dear little love,

I was thinking about love today; about how it changes shape depending on who it's for. There aren't many people I've truly loved.

I love your grandmother, your aunt, your uncle. Even Lou.

I suppose I love my dad too, in a strange, faraway kind of way, even though he left before I ever got the chance to know what loving him really meant.

As for your dad... I don't know anymore. Maybe I still love him. Maybe I'm just in love with the person I thought he was.

But you, I love you in a way that terrifies me. I'd walk through fire if it meant keeping you safe - without a second thought.

That's why I'm doing this; why I'm planning to see him.

It might be stupid. It might be brave. It's probably both.

Love,

Mumma

*P*aige sat on the old lounge in her favourite café, the cracked leather cushions smooth and luxurious. The air was rich with the scent of freshly ground coffee beans while intoxicating sweet smells - cinnamon maybe, or caramel - emanated from the kitchen. Outside, light rain pattered against the window, blurring the street view into a smudge of watercolour.

Her fingers held the warm mug on her lap, steam from her caffeine hit spiralling upwards before vanishing into the air. She watched it with an absent focus, her mind mentally preparing for the showdown with Elliot.

She cradled her bump, now hidden beneath a mustard-coloured dress that fell over her body like a soft veil. A tiny ladder had appeared in her stockings and she fought the urge to pull at it, just to see how far it would run.

Her daughter kicked sharply beneath her ribs, reminding her of her presence. Paige flinched, arching her back and pressing her hand gently against the swell. That one hurt.

"Stop being cheeky," she whispered with a smile, massaging the spot where her daughter was using her for soccer practice.

It was during this exchange that Elliot walked in. He saw her first. Like a moth to a flame, his eyes had been magnetically drawn to her the moment he entered the doorway. Her radiance dominated the room. In that instance, the hustle and bustle of the café faded into oblivion and his mind flooded with the memories of her that he had tried so long to forget. Paige. *His* Paige.

He ached for her; longed to feel her touch again - the warmth of her skin, the way her fingers would curl gently around his as though they were made for that specific purpose. More than anything, he ached to press his palm against the curve of her belly, to feel the soft flutter of life, to be a part of her future. At this, he woke from his dreamy trance, the harsh truths of reality hitting him like a tonne of bricks.

Wanting and having were worlds apart. Paige's baby wasn't his.

She looked up, sensing him like a shift in the air. Their eyes locked.

"Hi, Paige." Elliot finally let out.

Her smile, the one she had shared with her baby, disappeared, replaced now with a scowl cold enough to sting.

"Elliot."

His name on her tongue made his heart twitch. He used to love how she would pronounce it - soft, warm, teasing - but now, it felt like a slap. Cold; no tenderness. Just Elliot.

He took the seat across from her, and took in her beauty. Although she looked tired and unimpressed to be in his company, she was still the most stunning woman he had ever seen.

"Thanks for meeting me," he offered, rubbing his now sweating palms on the rough denim of his jeans.

She studied him as he spoke and, in a way that unnerved him, she smiled. Not with fondness, but with satisfaction. He looked like hell, and she liked that. It made her feel less alone in her own suffering.

"What did you want to talk about?" Her voice was officious and straight to the point causing him to flinch.

She rolled her eyes. "Could you hurry up? I don't have all day."

"Yeah, sorry..." He swallowed. "I guess I just wanted some closure."

"Closure?" she echoed, eyebrows arching. "Closure about what, exactly?"

"About us. I just..." He exhaled slowly, holding her gaze. "I just need to know why you did it."

His eyes flicked down to her belly just as the bump shifted, a tiny ripple silhouetted against the tight material.

Elliot held his breath. Was that the baby?

Paige followed his eye line and gently pressed her hand against the spot. A small foot had formed a perfect little bulge. With practised ease, she gave it a soft nudge until it retreated.

Elliot stared, awestruck.

In that one moment, something inside him cracked wide open.

"She's a bit active," Paige murmured distractedly, unable to hide the smile in her voice as her attention lingered on the baby.

For a split second, the tension lifted, but then she remembered his question and the warmth in her chest materialised back into a raging inferno.

"Why I did what?" she asked pointedly, levelling her gaze.

"Why you cheated on me," Elliot's voice dropped as the words left his mouth.

The words landed harder than he'd expected. He had said them in his head a thousand times, but saying them aloud ripped open a new wound.

Paige's face twisted. "Excuse me? I did not cheat on you," she snapped, voice rising.

"Yes, you did."

"No. I fucking didn't."

"With your publicist," he pushed. "What's his name?"

She blinked. "Jason?"

"Yeah. Him. You're pregnant with his baby."

There was a beat of stunned silence, followed by laughter.

Paige couldn't stop. She laughed, hysteria taking hold. She wiped at the tears that sprang to her eyes unbidden, even though it wasn't really that funny. The shock, mixed with her out of control hormones, her exhausted heart and the sheer absurdity of the accusation, broke her.

"Oh. My. God. That's good; that's really good," she managed to get out between breaths. "I mean… Jesus, Elliot!"

Elliot was stunned, taken aback by her unexpected reaction. "Why are you laughing?" he asked, wounded.

"Because that has to be the biggest load of shit I've ever heard," she retorted. Catching her breath, she continued, "Honestly, I wish it were his baby! Where on earth did you even get that idea? I thought I was the storyteller."

"I was told by someone who would know."

She scoffed. "Really? Who? Because unless you heard it from me or Jason, I wouldn't bet your life on it."

"I know it's true. This person wouldn't lie to me."

She narrowed her eyes, her smile gone. "Who told you this crap, Elliot?"

Before he could answer, a sharp pang stabbed through her stomach. Her breath hitched. She paused, hand on her belly and waited.

It passed.

She shook it off. She wasn't going to let him see her pain.

"Answer the question," she demanded.

"Someone..." Elliot muttered, eyes darting.

"Who is this someone?" Paige's voice sliced through the air.

"Just... someone I know. Why should I believe you?"

She didn't skip a step. "Why should you believe them?"

"Because he's my best friend!" he snapped.

Realisation flashed in her eyes like lightning. Her voice dropped to a low, dangerous register.

"Ahh... it was Shaun... wasn't it?"

Regretting his outburst, he tried to backtrack. "No," he lied.

Her tone sharpened, icy cold and precise. "Don't lie to me, Elliot. It was Shaun. Jesus Christ! I should have known!"

Another pang rolled through her abdomen, this one deeper, pulling her breath from her chest. She winced, placing a steady hand on her bump.

Elliot leaned forward. "Paige, are you okay?"

"I'm fine," she answered through gritted teeth. "Don't change the subject. Shaun fed you this bullshit, didn't he?"

"...Yes." His voice was small now, unsure.

Her fury flamed.

"Why the fuck would you believe a man who has spent years belittling you? Who showed up at my door after you left me and told me it was my fault?" Her voice shook with restrained rage.

"He doesn't treat me like shit! He's my best friend."

"Best friend?" she echoed, incredulous. "Okay. Let's talk about your best friend."

She pressed forward, eyes like steel. "Last year. Your birthday. Canada. Ring a bell?"

He blinked.

"You're telling me your best friend didn't push you into a frozen lake?" Her voice cracked with disbelief. "You nearly got hypothermia, Elliot. You were sick for weeks."

He was quiet.

Paige kept going. "He not only humiliated you, he almost killed you, but you still choose to believe him over me? Over your daughter?"

The silence between them stretched as Elliot searched his memory for the details.

All he remembered was slowly waking up to the ice, the shock and the laughter from the guys. Shaun had called it a joke. He'd laughed too, numbly, while shaking from the cold. He hadn't thought about it in months but now... he didn't know.

"It was a joke; an accident," Elliot replied weakly.

Paige's eyes narrowed. "Which one was it, Elliot? A joke or an accident?"

He opened his mouth, closed it. "Errr, both... no, umm, I don't know..."

But Paige wouldn't let him off the hook. She reeled off all the times Shaun had undermined him, insulted him or made choices for him. It was a long, confronting list, and hearing them catalogued in this way forced him to re-examine his interpretation of everything that had occurred in his past.

This included Lexus.

The last few weeks had been hell on earth. His marriage was a sham. Years ago he had promised himself that he'd never get divorced, yet now, here he was, seriously considering it. Every time he spoke to Shaun about his regrets, Shaun brushed things off and tried to talk him out of it - it'll work out; you're just overreacting;

these are normal relationship teething pains. But that morning, after opening yet another credit card bill and seeing the damage Lexus had done, he knew the truth. She was a money-hungry gold digger, and Shaun had handed her to him on a drunken platter with a smile.

"So you chose him over me." It wasn't a question, just a statement of truth. The sad truth.

Finally realising the gravity of the situation, Elliot's already fragile world came crashing down. In the blink of an eye he went from shock, guilt and humiliation through to sadness, anxiety and helplessness. He was broken.

"I'm sorry," he whispered, unable to face her..

Paige stared at him. "Sorry isn't good enough."

He looked up, eyes glassy. "So... does this mean... is she..."

"She is your daughter," Paige answered, locking eyes with him.

Elliot blinked. "My daughter?"

"Yes, you idiot," she huffed, just as another pain gripped her. Rising to her feet and clutching her belly, she gripped the edge of the table, trying to steady herself.

"We're having a daughter?" he repeated, stunned.

"Yes!" she snapped, the pain more intense now, undeniable.

Elliot jumped up. "Wait, please don't go! We have so much to talk about. So much to sort... "

"That'll have to wait," her voice wobbled with strain as she cut him short.

"What? Why?"

"Because I think our daughter's trying to make her appearance earlier than planned!" she said doubled over as the contraction took over.

It took a moment for the penny to drop; to understand why her face was contorted with pain and her hands white from knuckling the table.

"Oh my god," he breathed. "Okay okay." He moved to her side and threw an arm around her for support. "Which hospital?"

"Mount Sinai. On 98th."

He barely registered her words, only that she'd said 'our', which meant he wasn't being pushed away.

Minutes later, she was in his car, writhing in pain as the contractions tore through her. Elliot drove like the world was on fire, one hand gripping hers, knuckles tight.

"I'm so sorry, Paige," he whispered to himself as she clenched her jaw against another scream.

She heard it; felt the sincerity in it.

And despite everything, for the first time in a long while, she was grateful for Elliot.

CHAPTER TWENTY

Dear little love,

I did some googling and apparently unborn babies feel the emotions of their mothers through the placenta and umbilical cord. That would be interesting and kind of cool if I didn't feel the way I do.

I'm sorry you can feel all this chaos inside me. I'm trying so hard to be steady for you, but some days I feel like an imposter wearing human skin. I know I can't protect you from everything, but I'll try to make our world more peaceful before you get here.

I promise you that with all my heart.

Love,

Mumma

*P*aige huffed and puffed as Elliot pulled up to the front of the hospital. He slammed the car into park, skidding to a stop, pulling up mere centimetres before the vehicle in front - not that he cared. He sprinted around to her side just as another contraction took hold, folding her in half with a groan.

She clung to him, nails digging into his arm, each wave of pain stealing more of her breath. Fear had her by the throat.

It was too soon. Far too soon.

She was only thirty-three weeks. Not at the predicted thirty-four and nowhere near the ideal thirty-seven. Her chest tightened with every thought. As her anxiety spiked, so did the contractions - sharp, brutal, unrelenting.

Elliot half-dragged, half-carried her through the hospital doors, his eyes wild with panic. She stumbled, one hand clutching her stomach, the other swiping at the sweat on her brow between contractions.

He shoved his way to the front of the reception line.

"She needs help. Now!" he barked, voice cracking.

The nurse barely glanced up, unimpressed. "How far along is she? Who's her doctor?"

"Uhhh... " Elliot froze, mind blank. "Good question, I... I don't know."

The nurse raised an eyebrow, disdain in her eyes.

Elliot spun toward Paige, frantic. "Paige?"

Paige straightened just enough to rasp out, "My name is Paige Lawson. Thirty-three weeks. My OB is Dr Liam Baker." Her tone was calm and scrupulously polite, but her eyes betrayed her true feelings.

Elliot stepped back, feeling like a heel as a hot wave of shame burned up his neck. He didn't know how far along she was. Didn't even know her doctor's name. What kind of man doesn't know that? A real father would.

The nurse clacked away on her keyboard, fingers flying.

"Alright. I'm going to give Dr Baker a call and see what he wants to do," she said.

The moment the phone was at her ear, her tone shifted to syrupy and flirtatious.

"Hi, Dr Baker! It's Louise from Reception. How are you?" she cooed.

Paige narrowed her eyes.

"Oh, I'm good. Can't complain," the nurse giggled, twirling the cord around her finger. "Would love to see your pretty face around here more often... hahaha! Yes, coffee sounds... oh! Right. Why I'm calling..."

Paige ground her teeth. Focus, Louise!

"One of your patients is here. Paige Lawson." A pause. "Mmm. okay, got it. I'll send her right up."

She hung up and adjusted her blouse, smoothing her skirt like she was about to walk a runway.

"Dr Baker has requested you go straight up," she said, already turning her attention to the next person in line.

Paige rolled her eyes and waddled towards the elevator, clutching her bump with one hand and muttering to herself.

"Unbelievable!"

Elliot followed at her heels, guilt and tension written across every line of his face.

"What a stupid woman..." Elliot grumbled under his breath.

Paige let out a small laugh, which was broken by another deep groan as a contraction gripped her.

She leaned harder into Elliot, her fingers tightening on his arm as they waited for the elevator. Between breaths, she peeked up at him. His posture had changed. He was tense, alert and in hyper-protective mode.

This was something she had always admired about Elliot: when fear took over, he acted. Always had.

The elevator dinged. The doors slid open and before they could step in, someone came barrelling out.

Liam.

He stopped short, his eyes darting between Paige - pale, sweaty, wincing - and the man holding her.

"Paige?" he said, breathless. "Are you okay? What's happening?"

He moved to her side, slipping an arm around her back, guiding her away from Elliot and into the elevator with ease.

"I was out with Elliot and I started getting contrac--ahh..." Paige broke off mid sentence, her face contorting as the next wave hit.

Liam steadied her. "Breathe, Paige. You're doing great."

Elliot stood just inside the elevator, watching his replacement take over, suddenly feeling like a third wheel.

Liam shot him a look, eyes narrowing. "So... you're Elliot."

His tone made Elliot blink, but he nodded assent.

The elevator was silent but for Paige's breathing. The tension between the two men crackled and fizzed, so thick it was hard to ignore. It hung in the air and clung to the walls. Paige could have sworn it made her pain worse.

"What do we do? It's too early," she panted, searching Liam's face for answers but taking comfort from his calm demeanour.

His expression softened as he turned back to her. "We're going to get you in a bed, hook you up to the monitors and see what's going on. Once we know, we'll make a plan."

His voice deepened, low and warm. Anchoring. His eyes flicked briefly to her lips, before meeting hers again. Now wasn't the time - focus!

Paige dipped her head, her body trembling from the strain. Even in the lull between contractions, she ached all over, particularly down her lower back. She didn't know if it would help, but right this minute all she wanted was to lie down and close her eyes, pretend none of this was happening.

Liam turned his attention to Paige's former partner and, this time, there was no doubting his feelings. It was written all over his face. The look he gave him could not have been any colder.

He didn't know Elliot, but he hated what he'd done. And he didn't trust him near her now.

"You can go now," Liam said sharply, moving to help Paige out of the elevator.

"No thanks," Elliot replied. "I'll stay."

Liam bit his tongue but didn't argue: Paige was his priority.

Within minutes, although it felt like hours, the mother-to-be was lying in a hospital bed, machines beeping softly around her. There was a man on either side of her - Elliot to the left, Liam to the right.

"You need to calm down, Paige, your heart rate's elevated," Liam commented, eyes fixed on the monitor. His voice was clinical, his face unreadable.

Paige closed her eyes and used all her willpower to slow her breathing. The pain was manageable now, dulled by the morphine they'd administered on arrival, but her mind was racing.

What would it feel like to hold her daughter? Would she look like her or Elliot? Would she cry constantly or be one of those sleepy newborns who barely stirred?

Paige secretly hoped she'd have Elliot's eyes.

Those gorgeous eyes; deep green and flecked with gold. Depending on the day, his eyes either sparkled like emeralds or took on a warm honey hue. No matter her feelings for him these days, she could never quite shake the way those eyes made her feel.

Today, his smouldering eyes were a rich, forest green. They refused to leave Paige's face, and instead winced in tandem with her as a new wave of pain hit her. Elliot's chest tightened with every contraction, and he could only admire her bravery as she rode out each one with slow breaths and clenched fists. He didn't know much about pregnancy. Or labour. Or babies. But he knew enough to understand that 33 weeks was too soon.

He had taken an instant dislike to Liam and his proprietary air, but knew he needed him in this room. He couldn't stop sneaking quick looks at Liam, silently begging for reassurance. For answers. For something that said: They're okay. I won't lose them.

Then, without thinking, he reached out and took Paige's hand. To his surprise she let him. She squeezed it tightly, keeping her eyes closed and her breathing measured. The contact wasn't forced. It was grounding. Mutual.

Elliot slid his chair closer, lifted her hand to his lips, and pressed a soft kiss to her knuckles. Then he closed his eyes and made a wish. He wished for his family back; for all the pain of the last few months to vanish. He wished for the chance to love them right this time - the two of them… no, the three of them.

His silent prayer was interrupted by the low buzz of his phone; a technological intruder invading a private moment. Frustrated, he quickly smiled at Paige, and excused himself into the hall.

"I'll be right back."

The lights above buzzed faintly as he pulled the phone from his pocket, not even checking the screen before answering.

"Elliot, where are you?"

The sound of her voice scraped down his spine like broken glass… Lexus.

He grimaced before responding.

"I'm at the hospital."

"Hospital?" Her tone, as usual, was shrill and mocking. "Are you sick or are you just hungover again?"

He balled his fists, prepared for the reaction to come.

"Paige went into labour."

One. Two. Three. And then it came…

"What did you just say?" she hissed. "Tell me you're not at the hospital with that woman."

"Yes, I am," Elliot snapped. "She's thirty-three weeks, Lexus. Too early. And I'm not about to walk away from her. Or from my kid."

"Your kid?" she spat, frothing with rage. "She told you that baby wasn't even yours! You're unbelievable. Do you know how humili-ating this is for me? Do you know what people will say if they find out where you are right now? My husband, standing next to his ex, while she pops out another man's bastard child."

The venom in her words hit him like acid. His pulse thundered.

"I don't care what anyone says," he shot back. "I care about her. I care about that baby. And nothing you say is going to keep me away."

The silence that followed was colder than her rage.

"You'll regret this," she said finally, her voice poisonous. "Don't think for a second I won't make you pay for embarrassing me like this."

He ended the call before she could finish and, hands shaking, he shoved the phone deep into his pocket. When he stepped back into the room, the warmth was gone. Liam eyeballed him, hard as steel, the kind of look that didn't just warn, it threatened. Paige, meanwhile, was watching him from the bed, her expression curious but unreadable.

"Who was that?" she asked, her voice deceptively light.

"Just my agent," Elliot lied smoothly, forcing a shrug. "Nothing important."

Her brow furrowed ever so slightly, as if she wasn't convinced. Liam, however, wasn't nearly as subtle. He crossed his arms over his chest, every inch of him radiating suspicion.

"Funny," he said evenly. "Most agents don't scream like banshees over the phone."

Elliot's throat went dry. He forced a thin smile, but his stomach churned. He turned to face Liam, seizing the only escape available to him. "How's everything going, Doc?"

The scowl Liam gave him said it all; he wasn't buying it. He was prepared to push his advantage, but was distracted by Paige, whose focus had shifted back to her baby.

"Well, Liam, what's happening?" she queried tentatively.

Liam sat beside her, his face drawn. He reached for her hand, gently stroking her fingers, soothing her with his touch. The action didn't go unnoticed by Elliot. In response his heart experienced something he hadn't felt for a long time - possessiveness and jealousy.

He swallowed hard as he registered that she had called him Liam. They were familiar; comfortable. This man had been there for Paige when Elliot hadn't and the idea of that sat rotten in his stomach, curdling into something dark and unwelcome. He had no right to feel that way, after all it was his actions that had brought them here.

Liam spoke softly. "I'm sorry, Paige, but you really are in labour."

She closed her eyes, throat tightening. Her lids trembled, straining against the tears which threatened to break through. Even though a part of her knew it was illogical, Paige had been holding out hope that this was just a scare, a false alarm. The truth was now staring down at her - it was real. She had failed to do the one thing she was supposed to do: carry her baby to term. Protect her. Keep her safe.

Liam's voice softened further, responding to her unasked questions. "I'm going to give you medication to slow the contractions. I don't expect it to stop them entirely, but it should buy us some time. Over the next twenty-four hours, we'll give you two steroid shots. They'll help accelerate the baby's lung development."

Paige nodded faintly, trying to keep her composure. The clinical tone was meant to console her, reinforce she was in the best place for her unborn child and in the safest hands, but she could feel the weight of what he wasn't saying - that they were now counting down to the baby's birth in hours, not months.

Observing the action like a stranger in his own life, Elliot felt out of place. His role had been reduced from an active participant to a trespasser. What hurt most was feeling that shift and being unable to do anything to stop it.

For there was a certain bond here between Paige and her doctor; something he couldn't name but could feel. There was a vibe, a chemistry that lingered. Like an ocean's undercurrent, it pulled them away from him. It was in the quiet between their words; in the way Liam's eyes hovered just a tad too long on her face; in the way Paige's breathing steadied when his hand brushed hers.

Paige opened her eyes again, fixing her attention on the far wall, her voice clipped and urgent.

"Someone needs to call my mum and tell her what's going on," she said. "And I need my hospital bag. It's by the door at home. I wasn't ready... I didn't think... "

Her words stalled as the brutal reality pressed in from all sides. Her mind spun in a tangle of to-do lists, what-ifs, and jagged fears, each one tripping over the next.

"I'll get one of the nurses to make the call," Liam assured her gently. "And we'll have your things brought here. Is there anything else you'd like?"

Paige paused, securing their attention before saying, "I'd love a burger," in a deadpan voice.

To her pleasant surprise - yes, pleasant - both men laughed out loud; a real laugh, quick and warm, cutting the tension in the room. Even now, in the midst of premature labour, her pregnancy cravings still knew how to make themselves heard.

"I'm sorry, Paige," Liam said between chuckles. "You can't eat in case we need to take you for an emergency caesarean."

His voice remained neutral, obscuring the veneer of firmness hiding below. It was the sort of steadiness you'd want from someone holding your baby's life in their hands. As he spoke, his thumb continued its merry dance across the back of her hand, slow and hypnotic. For a long time.

Abruptly, Liam cleared his throat and jumped up, as if suddenly conscious of their public show of intimacy. "I'll let the nurse know."

He gave Paige one last glance before stepping out, Elliot's withering glare burning into his back like a hot brand. The door clicked shut. Silence fell heavy.

Elliot's phone buzzed angrily in his pocket. He pulled it out to see a flood of missed calls and furious texts from Lexus, each one more frantic than the last. He stared at the screen for a moment, thumb hovering over the reply. Then he locked it without responding.

He didn't care.

Not now.

Paige needed him.

And for the first time in a long time, he knew exactly where he belonged.

CHAPTER TWENTY ONE

Dear little love,
I couldn't get out of bed today.
There was no point.
Why try?
Love,
Mumma

Elliot

Elliot shuffled his chair closer to the hospital bed, the warmth of his body brushing the space beside her.

Being so close to her dragged him back to countless memories he thought he'd buried for good. Nights on the couch with her head in his lap. Mornings tangled in sheets, her fingers brushing absent-minded circles on his arm like she couldn't stand not to be touching him. Back then, it had been so natural. So constant. As if she needed him as much as he needed her.

It had been so long since he'd felt her warmth. So long since he'd let himself remember. And now, this simple brush of skin sparked a wildfire, a surging inferno, in places he thought had gone numb.

His gaze wandered to the monitor. The numbers were climbing again - the glowing green numbers signalling her increasing heart rate, her growing anxiety.

"It's okay, Paige," he whispered, forcing his voice calm when his own nerves frayed. "You're okay. Just breathe for me. Nice and slow."

She closed her eyes, fighting the panic clawing at her chest, but her breath came sharp and uneven. Then her voice broke.

"I don't want a C-section." The words came out in a rush, cracking in the middle. Her eyes flew open, wide and wet, desperate. The fear inside them shattered something deep in him.

He leaned forward, clutching her hand tighter, his thumb still stroking. "I know. I know. It'll be okay. I swear it will." His voice shook with a promise he wasn't sure he'd be able to keep.

Without thinking, he reached up and brushed the damp strands of hair from her face. She leaned into his palm, just the faintest tilt of her head, just enough to feel him.

That tiny motion hit him like a sledgehammer. It was such a small gesture, so subtle, yet it made his chest seize, his breath catch and his hope flicker back to life.

Maybe… just maybe, they could still be something.

"Will you distract me?" she asked faintly.

He didn't even hesitate. "Of course. What do you want me to do?"

"I think we need to talk about our situation."

Elliot was not prepared for that; not now. He stiffened, the muscles in his jaw tightening like a wire pulled too taut.

"No," he said gently, but leaving no room for negotiation. "That'll just stress you out more. We don't want to bring on more contractions."

"I know," she said, offering a wry smile. "But not knowing where we stand; it's been driving me crazy for months. I can't keep living like this."

She shifted slightly on the bed, giggling. "Plus, I'm doped up on morphine so I probably won't yell at you."

He gave a soft chuckle in return, but the smile didn't reach his eyes. Inside, his chest ached.

She was joking - kind of - but her gaze was unflinching; her expression serious.

She wasn't asking for closure. She was asking for the truth.

And maybe… for hope.

"Okay," Elliot said at last, voice low. "But if you start to get upset again, or your heart rate spikes too high, we stop. Immediately."

He held her eyes as he said it, not as a demand, but as a promise. He was giving her control. And if he had any hope of getting his family back, this was where it started.

Paige nodded. "That's fair."

More silence settled between them. He knew it was up to him to make the first move.

"What do you want to talk about?" he asked timidly.

Her answer came without hesitation.

"Why did you leave me?"

Her voice cracked on the last word, pain spilling through it like a wound that had never fully closed.

Elliot couldn't stand hearing the agony in her voice, knowing he was the cause of anguish. His foot tapped once against the linoleum before stilling. He should have known she'd go straight for the jugular.

"I honestly don't know," he admitted, his voice shaking. "I didn't have one big reason. Just… little ones that festered."

As much as he wanted to, he couldn't look at her while he exposed his ugly truth. Even so, he could feel her eyes locked on him, demanding, pleading for an answer that would make sense of the mess.

"For weeks, I felt like you were putting me last; like you were replacing me with the book you were writing," he tried to explain.

"I know how selfish that sounds; I know how hard you worked, but it felt like you didn't see me anymore."

Paige did not move at all, not wanting to break his momentum. She needed answers. She deserved answers.

"I'd just come back from eight weeks of filming in LA and when I walked in the door, all you talked about was your book. You didn't ask how I was. You didn't say you missed me. Then I started shooting again in New York and… you never once asked about the project. You were in meetings or locked in the study, always busy. We stopped going out. We stopped being… us. I guess I let that eat away at me."

His voice dropped lower, like it shamed him to say it out loud. "Shaun didn't help. He told me you were over me; that you were just waiting for the right moment to leave."

Paige's fingers curled into the sheets, squeezing them for all she was worth.

"I know now that wasn't true," Elliot rushed out. "He was baiting me, pushing buttons, but at the time I believed him."

How it pained him to admit those words! He rubbed his palms together, the sound rough in the quiet room.

"And then there was the woman I worked with. God, I can't even remember her name…"

"Heather," Paige said flatly. "Her name was Heather."

Elliot winced like she'd struck him. "Right. Heather."

He finally looked at her and what he saw made his throat close - sadness, heartbreak and something…harder…underneath.

"She was kind. That's all. But Shaun, he hyped her up. Made it sound like she was into me; like she wanted me. I was so desperate for something - any kind of affection - that I let it get in my head. I was starving, Paige. For attention. For you."

His voice cracked on her name.

"She wasn't special. She was just there. And I was stupid enough to mistake that for something more."

Paige felt compelled to speak up; to share her truth.

"You know you never came second to my book," she affirmed with a steady voice. "Not once. Never."

Elliot nodded, guilt pressing down like lead. "I know that now. I really do."

He swallowed. "I think… I was just being too needy. And maybe… maybe I was jealous of you. Of your success."

Paige blinked. "You were jealous of me?"

"I think so. Yeah." He shifted uncomfortably. "You've got this… effortless talent. People love your work. You don't have to chase it - it comes to you. And me? I'm still fighting for auditions, still working my ass off to stay relevant. It felt like you were surpassing me; like you were leaving me behind."

She said nothing.

"I, uh… I actually started seeing a therapist last week," he added, the words awkward on his tongue.

Her eyebrows lifted in surprise. "You did?"

"Yeah. Only had one session, but it… it was eye-opening. He said some of what I'm feeling - the insecurity, the fear - might come from the abandonment stuff with my dad."

His voice cracked slightly. "It makes sense, I guess."

Paige nodded. "Yeah. It does."

"So I think I was just… waiting for you to leave me," Elliot admitted. "And when I thought you would, I panicked. I left first so it would hurt less."

The truth settled between them with the weight of something long avoided.

"Okay…" she said slowly. "But that still doesn't explain why you came back into my life to help with the baby… and then vanished again right before an important appointment."

Elliot exhaled. "I know. That was the worst of it."

He rubbed his hands together again before stopping suddenly, his fingers flexing and relaxing repeatedly. "Shaun called me the day before that appointment and asked to meet me for lunch."

Paige's expression hardened. "And he told you the baby wasn't yours."

Elliot nodded. "Yeah. He said you were sleeping with your publicist; that it had been going on for a while."

Paige closed her eyes and shook her head slowly, the frustration and disbelief radiating off her in waves.

Of course Shaun had said that. And of course Elliot had believed him.

"You're a fucking idiot, Elliot," she snapped, her voice sharp and wounded.

Before he could respond, the monitor beside them began to beep faster - her heart rate climbing.

Elliot's face drained of colour. "Paige!"

"Shit! Paige, okay, breathe. You've got to calm down."

He reached for her hand again, gently. "We said if it got too much, we'd stop. Just breathe, alright? Please."

"Don't tell me to calm down!" Paige retorted, her voice raw with fury. "Why the hell would you believe him? Shaun is a liar! A stupid, fucking, piss weak idiot! Did you have no trust in me? Not even a little?!"

Her words hit like shrapnel, one after another, each sharper than the last - and still, Elliot didn't flinch.

"I'm sorry!" he cried. "I am so damn sorry. You have no idea how sorry I am. Please, Paige, please calm down. For her."

His hands reached forward, trembling, and gently rested on her belly.

Her breath hitched.

The rage in her chest collapsed like a wave crashing onto shore, giving way to something far more potent. Grief. Relief. Release.

First came the tears.

She stared at his large hands, shaking and resting against the curve of her stomach. Their daughter, reminding them of her existence, kicked softly beneath his touch.

Elliot's own eyes welled as he felt the smallest movement under his palms - a flutter. His heart clenched.

His daughter.

Paige blinked through her tears, watching the man she'd once loved more than life itself be utterly undone by the simplest of contacts.

Something shifted inside her. A flicker. A spark. The one she thought she'd buried months ago.

It wasn't gone. It had just been waiting.

Suspended in a moment too fragile to risk, they remained entwined - the three of them - unwilling to let go.

And then Elliot looked up.

His eyes met hers - desperate, full of love.

"I love you, Paige," he whispered.

CHAPTER TWENTY TWO

Dear little love,

I feel like all I do is promise you things and not overly deliver, but here's another one.

I promise to love you through your mistakes. I promise not to judge you or desert you when you're in need. I promise to have your back - no matter where we end up - together or not.

Love,

Mumma

Paige lay before him, Elliot's hand warm against her stomach, tears shimmering in his eyes.

"I love you, Paige."

The words hung in the air, sharp and paralyzing.

She froze. Couldn't move. Couldn't breathe. Her heart pounded, caught between disbelief and the part of her that had been waiting, no, aching, to hear them again. Did he mean it? Was it real? And what was she supposed to do with it now?

Heat radiated from his palm over her belly, spreading through her like dawn breaking across her skin. Her pulse jumped, panic threatening to engulf her. She needed to calm down, but before she could say a word, a sharp kick jolted beneath Elliot's hand.

Paige was used to the jabs. Not so Elliot; this was the first time their daughter had ever reached for him.

His expression crumbled. Overwhelmed, he slid to his knees at her bedside, his face level with her bump. He pressed his lips against her skin, again and again, his voice cracking with each word.

"I'm sorry… God, I'm so sorry. I wasn't there. I let you down. I let them take me away. I should've fought for you; for both of you. Please forgive me. I love you. I've never stopped loving you."

The words tore from him in sobs, spilling like a confession. Paige could hardly believe this outpouring of emotion. Something inside her shifted and cracked wide open.

It was love. She still loved him. God help her, she did.

As if he felt her admission, Elliot lifted his tear-streaked face, eyes blazing with hope, and kissed her.

It was like a match to gasoline.

Fire.

Every nerve lit up as his mouth claimed hers, his cologne mixing with the salt of his tears. She didn't think. She couldn't. Her body betrayed her, leaning in, answering him. She kissed him back. Hard.

She knew it was wrong; knew it was reckless. None of it mattered though. She kissed him like he was oxygen and he kissed her like she was the only thing that had ever mattered. The months apart melted away. Her fingers fisted in his shirt, dragging him closer. Between them, their daughter kicked wildly, insistent, as if she refused to be forgotten at this moment.

Elliot smiled against her lips, and Paige's heart fluttered just like it used to.

Neither of them noticed the shadow filling the doorway.

"What the fuck do you think you're doing with my husband?!"

The screech shattered the moment like glass. Paige jolted, her heart leaping into her throat. Elliot tore himself away, guilt and confusion written across his face.

Lexus filled the doorway like a storm, wild-eyed, hands waving, her blonde locks frizzing with fury.

Paige was paralysed with shock. Her body went rigid, every nerve screaming. Elliot watched his wife closely as though he could not believe she were real.

"Lexus, what are you doing here?"

"I thought it was a little too convenient that you were playing house in a hospital with your ex, so I came to check. Surprise!" she spat, stomping into the room.

She folded her arms, her glare slicing across the bed. "I should have known."

Paige's stomach twisted violently. For one fleeting, beautiful minute she had let herself imagine Elliot was hers again. But that world had never included Lexus.

"There are, like, fifty hospitals in New York," Elliot muttered. "How the hell did you even find us?"

"Sixty two," Lexus corrected smugly. "And it wasn't hard. I tracked your phone."

He blinked, stunned. "You tracked me?"

She tilted her chin defiantly. "What was I supposed to do? You're here with that lying bitch, carrying some other guy's baby. How am I supposed to trust you?!"

Her voice rose higher with each word until it rattled the white sterile walls. Storming closer to the bed with eyes blazing, the threat was imminent..

Paige's throat went dry; she couldn't speak. Trapped in the bed, she tensed, too sore and too afraid to move.

Elliot stepped in front of her, shoulders squared. "Lexus! Stop! You need to leave!"

"Absolutely not." Her voice dripped venom. "She needs to learn her place. You think you can spread your legs, sleep with him and steal him back? You can't. He's mine, you slut."

"Enough!" Elliot barked, his voice cracking the air like a whip.

But Lexus only leaned closer, her rage spilling unchecked.

"Take your bastard baby and fuck off!" she screamed. "He doesn't want you. He loves me. I'm the one with the ring, remember?"

Her smile was twisted, victorious. "How does it feel, Paige? Knowing he's been sleeping with me every night, waking up next to me in our bed? Making love to me?"

Every word landed like a blade. Paige's chest heaved, her stomach rolling as the baby kicked hard, unsettled by the chaos.

Elliot surged forward, grabbing Lexus by the arm and shoving her towards the door.

"That's enough, Lexus!"

She thrashed violently, unable to stop the hateful vitriol from leaving her mouth.

"He never loved you!" she howled. "Never! He didn't then, and he won't now. You're just some pathetic little girl who thought getting pregnant would trap him. How's that working out for you?!"

Something inside Paige broke.

"He might be married to you," she shot back with an unwavering voice, "but he will always choose me."

That was the breaking point.

Lexus lunged.

Security had barely reached the room when she ripped free of Elliot's grip and hurled herself forward, shrieking like a banshee.

Her end goal in sight, she closed her hand around Paige's IV line and yanked.

The room descended into chaos. Paige's scream tore through the ward as the needle was ripped from her arm. Blood sprayed across her gown, splattering the sheets and dotting the floor like a Jackson Pollock art piece. The equipment that had been checking on her daughter's vitals beeped and buzzed and flashed, issuing its brazen warnings.

"Get her out of here!" a nurse bellowed, applying gauze with pressure against Paige's bleeding arm while another shoved Elliot back.

Security wrestled Lexus into the hall, dragging her away kicking and screaming her voice echoing like a curse down the corridor.

"You'll regret this! He doesn't love you! He never did!"

Paige sobbed, clutching her belly, terror strangling her. Nurses swarmed her bed, their voices sharp and urgent.

And Elliot? In the face of his world collapsing around him, he stood still; pale and wide-eyed, taking in the blood-soaked bed. A sea of crimson pooled beneath Paige, warm and terrifying, spreading fast. Her body shook with ragged gasps, contractions sharpened by fear. The monitor screamed in frantic succession.

Her eyes found Elliot's. Wide. Shaking. Pleading.

Stay. Please. Stay.

In that look, she begged him to be her anchor.

And Elliot?

He saw it all.

The woman he had loved, bleeding out before him. The child he had made, fighting to hold on. The family he could have had, slipping away.

His chest constricted. His hand twitched, reaching for her. Almost.

And then he heard it. A scream from the hallway. Lexus.

His jaw clenched. His feet betrayed him.

Elliot turned, leaving the room, chasing the voice of the mistake he once called a promise

CHAPTER TWENTY THREE

Paige lay in the hospital bed, writhing as another contraction tore through her body. Nurses hovered, their voices calm, trying to steady the bleeding in her arm where Lexus had yanked the IV. The monitors sang their song next to her. The metallic smell of blood filled the air.

Perspiration dampened her hairline, her skin clammy, her gown soaked through.

Her chest rose and fell at pace, panic setting up home in her throat. The contractions weren't just painful, they were relentless, threatening to rip her daughter from the safety of her womb before she was ready.

How could she have been so stupid?

Her tears burnt hot trails down her face. She couldn't tell whether they came from the sharp ache in her body or the deeper wound inside her chest. Both felt unbearable.

The bleeding slowed. The chaos ebbed. Three nurses remained, hovering like sentinels, keeping an eye on her from a safe distance. One of them crouched by her side, her kind eyes offering solace as she reached out to pat Paige's arm.

"Do you need anything, honey?" she asked gently.

Paige's lips barely moved. "I want my mum."

As if the words themselves were an invocation, the door burst open.

Theresa rushed inside, her eyes wide, a lioness in search of her cub. A hospital bag hung off one shoulder, zip undone and some blue and white pyjamas on display. Behind her came Grace, pale with worry, and Jasper, posture rigid, bracing for a fight.

"What happened? Is everything okay?" Theresa demanded, making a beeline for her daughter's side.

Paige blinked up at her through glassy eyes. Her throat caught as she whispered, "He came back."

The words fell like stones in the room.

Theresa froze, her hand tightening on the bed rail. Grace let out a small gasp, pressing her fingers to her mouth. Jasper's brows furrowed, confusion hardening into something darker.

"He came back?" Grace echoed softly, as if she wasn't sure she had heard right.

"Yes." Paige swallowed, her voice trembling. "He said he loved me. He explained everything about why he left."

"Don't tell me you believed his crap," Jasper snapped, his tolerance for Elliot quite low.

Paige flinched, curling into herself as if his words had landed like a blow.

"I think he means it," she whispered with certainty.

"How can you think that?" Jasper's voice rose, raw with disbelief. "He left you, Paige. Without a word. He ghosted you and then married someone else. How the hell is that love?"

Paige's lips parted, her chest tightening, but she couldn't form the words to fight back. Her eyes brimmed with tears.

"We kissed," she admitted, the words escaping like a confession. "It felt like nothing had changed. He put his hand on my belly and she kicked, and he just started crying. He apologised over and over. He said Shaun lied, about me, about the baby. I think he really does love me."

Jasper let out a cynical laugh, running a hand through his hair as he started pacing the small room. His boots struck the linoleum with heavy thuds, each step an echo of pent-up frustration.

"Yeah? And what's to stop him from doing it again?" he demanded. "What happens the next time Shaun decides to stir shit up? Or someone tells him something he doesn't want to hear? You'll be left again. With a baby. Alone."

"Jasper…" Theresa warned, her tone gentle and determined.

"No, Mum." He whipped around, his eyes blazing. "This is the time to say it. She's lying here because of him. She's bleeding, terrified, in preterm labour because of the mess he created. If he believed those lies once, he'll believe them again. That's the plain and simple truth."

The room felt heavy. His words hung in the air, refusing to be ignored. She wanted to argue with Jasper, to shout at him, but the truth gnawed at her.

"Jasper!" Grace admonished, her melodic voice sharper than usual. She stepped forward, trying to catch his arm, but he shook her off.

Her eyes glistened, torn between siding with her sister and understanding her twin's fury. She had always been the peacekeeper, the one who could hold two truths at once, but this was too much even for her.

"Fuck that!" Jasper's voice cracked. He jabbed a finger toward Paige. "I can't watch her do this again."

His face twisted, pain breaking through the anger. He turned to Paige, his voice shattering. "You almost killed yourself, Paige. Do you remember that? You stood on a balcony ready to jump because of him, and now you're here again - bleeding and terrified - because of him. When will you learn?"

Listening to the monitors beep steadily, each note a metronome to her pounding heart, Paige reached out a trembling hand.

"Jasper..."

But he was already moving.

"Fuck this." His voice was broken now, jagged. "I'm done."

The slamming door reverberated around the room, causing the machines to spike and flutter. The nurses shifted uneasily, gazes alternating between Paige and the door as if waiting for the next explosion in this melodrama,

Grace, her hand half-lifted as if she could still pull him back, turned to Paige, her voice breaking. "I'm sorry. He's just scared. We all are."

Theresa leaned closer, brushing loose tendrils from her daughter's temple. Her voice was steady, but her eyes glistened. "We'll get through this, darling - one way or another. We'll get through it."

For the first time in a long time, Paige just didn't know if they would. She wondered if her brother might be right. She opened her eyes slowly to see Grace and Theresa exchange a loaded look. Grace gave a soft nod and followed after her brother, leaving their mother behind.

Theresa turned to her daughter and sat down beside the bed. She didn't speak, not yet, simply reaching for Paige's hand and humming the same lullaby she used to sing when Paige was little. That gentle tune, accompanied by all its happy memories, settled on them like a warm blanket.

Despite everything, Paige felt at peace in that moment. Her mother's voice carried her back to childhood nights when comfort was as simple as a song. Theresa didn't need to say anything aloud: this wasn't the time for judgment; not when her daughter needed support.

The contractions had eased, dulled by the medication. The first steroid shot had been administered, the new IV line bandaged neatly and the monitors beside her bed now behaved themselves, at long last beeping their steady, reassuring rhythm. The sting of fear hadn't disappeared completely, but it had loosened its grip.

As exhaustion overtook her, Paige dozed off. Her sleep was dreamless, but it provided a much-need small reprieve from the storm. Paige's hand remained loosely curled in her mother's, her chest rising and falling in shallow, even breaths.

She didn't hear her mother go. She didn't stir when the door creaked open.

Nor did she notice the figure who slipped quietly into the room.

Elliot

Elliot stormed down the hallway after Lexus, no longer ruled by fear but by white hot rage.

"What the fuck is your problem?" he barked as soon as they were alone.

Lexus spun on her heel, eyes flashing. "What's wrong with me? How about what's wrong with you?"

"She needs me!" Elliot shouted. "She's having my baby!"

"It's not your baby!" she spat.

"Yes. It. Is," he growled through clenched teeth. If he were a cartoon, steam would have been pouring from his ears.

"She cheated on you. You said so yourself."

"I was wrong," he snapped. "I made a mistake."

"Oh please." She let out a mocking laugh. "What are you going to do? Go crawling back and pretend none of this ever happened? Bit hard, considering you've got a wife, dickhead."

She emphasized wife like it was a crown she had won. A title she wore with pride.

"Not for long," Elliot shot back. "I want a divorce."

Lexus raised an eyebrow, unfazed. Crossing her arms, she smirked, "Not gonna happen."

"Oh, it will happen," Elliot growled, stepping closer. "I don't love you. I never did. You were a mistake. A drunken, life-ruining mistake."

He hoped the words would wound her enough to end this, but she stood there, smug and unmoved.

"I don't care," she said coolly. "I'm not divorcing you."

"Yes, you will," he said with frustration. "Take everything, I don't care -the apartment, the money, everything. Just leave me and Paige alone."

Lexus tilted her head and shrugged. "Hmm, no thanks. I appreciate the offer but … I do think I want the baby."

Elliot's blood ran cold.

"What?"

"Well, you are my husband. If that baby is yours, I could claim Paige was our surrogate; you know, one who went back on our agreement. Happens all the time," she said conversationally.

Her tone was terrifyingly casual, like she was discussing brunch.

"You can't do that," he whispered.

She smiled. "Oh, I wouldn't win, but the court process would be long, costly and stressful. Do you really think Paige would stick around through all of that?"

He felt like he had been kicked in the stomach.

"I could get some evidence forged," she added with a wink. "I know a guy."

Elliot could not believe what he was hearing. He had never heard anything so duplicitous or pointedly cruel in all his life. He clutched at his chest, breath caught in his throat. She was threatening his child. His daughter.

"She's got nothing to do with you," he rasped.

Lexus ignored him, already turning away. Her heels clacked like gunshots on the tile. "Shaun said I would have fun with you; I just didn't think I'd be this entertained," she said with a laugh.

With that she was gone, her cackle echoing behind her like a villain from a nightmare.

Elliot was reeling. She can't do this. She wouldn't. But even as he told himself that, dread twisted inside him.

And that's when it happened.

A shift in the air. A roar tearing through the corridor. He turned just in time to feel a solid crack explode across his face. Pain shot behind his eyes. He hit the floor hard, the world tilting, spinning. Before he could register what was happening, someone was on top of him, fists flying, obscenities pouring down like rain.

"You bastard! You piece of shit!" the voice screamed.

Strong hands grabbed the attacker and pulled them off. Nearby strangers rushed to help Elliot, pressing tissues and napkins to his bleeding nose, steadying him as he struggled upright.

Dazed, heart pounding, he blinked through the haze.

And then he saw who had hit him.

His heart broke all over again.

CHAPTER TWENTY FOUR

Dear little love,

Things have been quiet lately. No tears. No panic. Just stillness.

Is that peace or exhaustion pretending to be peace? I'm not sure yet.

I made a list of small things that make me happy: the smell of rain, tea that's still hot, feeling you kick.

The last one is my favourite.

Love,

Mumma

Paige

Theresa had only been gone a moment, just long enough for someone else to slip into the room.

The room was hushed, filled only with the low hum of machines and the faint shuffle of nurses beyond the door. Paige drifted in and out of medicated sleep, stirring not when a chair scraped softly against the floor nor when a quiet figure lowered themselves into it.

For a few moments, the figure simply watched. Paige's face looked softer in sleep, almost peaceful, her lips parted as though she were mid-sigh. The lines of tension that had etched themselves into her features over the last few months had eased.

As if sensing the weight of the gaze on her, Paige started to wake. Her lashes fluttered against her cheeks and, as her vision adjusted to the light, her tired eyes widened at the sight before her.

"Hi…" she whispered, her voice thick with exhaustion.

"Hello, mia cara," Rosa said softly.

Her voice cracked at the edges, not from age, but from something far more heart-wrenching - regret.

Instinctively rubbing at her face, Paige was surprised to find her cheeks damp.

"Are you okay?" she asked, her brows knitting together.

That was all it took.

The simple question broke Rosa. Her composure splintered, the proud, polished woman dissolving as the tears she had buried for months spilled over. At first they came in small tremors, then sobs so full-bodied they shook her shoulders. She covered her face with her hands, unable to look at Paige.

"I'm so sorry, cara," she choked out between cries. "I am so, so sorry."

Paige blinked, stunned. Of all the emotions she expected today, this wasn't one of them.

"Sorry for what?" she asked tentatively.

Rosa lifted her face, her eyes red and pleading. "For not being there. For not standing up for you or the baby. I should have put Elio in his place. I should have fought harder for the truth, but I was scared. He's my baby… and I didn't want to lose him."

Paige swallowed slowly, taking in the raw honesty in Rosa's eyes.

"It's okay," she murmured, though the words felt thin on her tongue.

"No," Rosa said firmly, shaking her head. "It isn't okay. He loves you, Paige. He really does. More than you probably realise. Every time I mentioned your name, I saw something inside him die. And in its place came someone I didn't recognize."

Her voice faltered, and fresh tears filled her eyes.

"These last few months have destroyed him. He lashes out, he isolates himself, he pushes everyone away."

"Everyone but Shaun," Paige mumbled bitterly.

Rosa's face darkened instantly, her refined features hardening like stone. "Do not even mention that man."

The venom in her tone startled Paige. For once, Rosa didn't look elegant or composed, she looked wild, a mother bear about to protect her cub, fury flashing like claws.

"I don't particularly like him either," Paige admitted, attempting a small smile to cut through the tension.

However Rosa wasn't finished.

"I'm sure he is behind all of this - the lies, the distance, that woman who somehow has gotten her talons into my son."

Paige's eyes widened at the sudden fire in Rosa's voice.

"She's ruined him," Rosa said, her words shaking with rage. "I tried to fight it, I really did. But she is poison. Evil, through and through. Just like Shaun."

"Yeah," Paige said softly, her hand drifting to her stomach. "She is. She was just here."

Rosa's expression snapped from rage to alarm. Leaning forward quickly, her hand gripped the side of the bed. "She was? What did she do? How did she know you were here?"

"I don't know," Paige admitted, her voice small. Squinting at Rosa, she turned the question back. "How did you know?"

"Your mother called me," Rosa said with a weary smile. "We have kept in touch these last few months. I wanted to find some way... any way... to stay involved with the baby. Your mum has been wonderful. Strong, level-headed, everything I am not. She is one of a kind."

Her eyes grew glassy again, her voice catching.

"That is how I know my little grandbaby is in the best hands... because you were raised by one of the best. I am so proud of you, Paige. So proud. And I hope... even if you still have hurt feelings toward me, or towards Elio, that you will let me be a part of her life."

The vulnerability in Rosa's voice gave Paige pause.

She wasn't sure what she felt. She didn't know where she stood with Elliot or what tomorrow would bring. Her only focus now was carrying her daughter safely into the world. Still, she gave Rosa the answer she was searching for.

"Sure."

Rosa's entire face lit up. A bright, wide smile bloomed, softening her tired features. She reached out and squeezed Paige's hand, her grip surprisingly firm. Words spilled out of her in a rush, questions about the pregnancy, about the baby's name, about cravings and nursery themes.

She was already planning a future Paige hadn't dared to picture yet.

Elliot

Downstairs, Elliot stood with blood pouring from his nose, clutching his face as he stared at the last person he ever expected to hit him. The copper taste filled his mouth. His vision blurred at the edges.

"Jasper! What have you done?" Grace cried, rushing forward to her brother's side as strangers held him back. Straining against their hold,

Jasper clenched and unclenched his fists, his body heaving with the effort to break free.

"He deserved it!" Jasper bellowed, his voice ragged with rage. "He's the scum of the earth, Grace. And you know it!"

The words sliced through Elliot, harsher than the sting in his face. His heart cracked at the fury in Jasper's voice, because it wasn't just anger. It was pain, betrayal.

"Jas… I'm sorry," Elliot managed, his voice muffled by the blood and tissues someone had shoved into his hand. His chest heaved, his ribs aching as shame pressed down like a weight.

"No! It's too late for that!" Jasper's eyes burned as he tried again to surge forward. "You deserted her. You deserted all of us! Did we mean nothing to you?" His voice broke mid-shout, grief laced into every syllable. "We took you in, treated you like family and you betrayed us."

The words gutted him.

Elliot's departure from Paige's life has affected the whole family, Elliot included. As an only child, he had never known the messy, fierce devotion of siblings. Until he'd met Jasper, that is.. From the moment they'd been introduced, it had been easy. They had shared long nights arguing about movies, traded sarcastic texts during family dinners, even planned a ridiculous cross-country road trip they never got to take. Jasper had been the brother Elliot never had; the brother he had secretly always wanted.

And now, here he was, fists raised, eyes wild, calling him scum.

"I'm sorry," Elliot said again, quieter this time. The words felt useless, flimsy, against the storm in front of him.

"Too bad!" Jasper's face twisted. "We trusted you. We loved you like our own blood. What a mistake that was."

Elliot's head hung low, shame coursing through him. His nose throbbed, his chest burned and still he could not find the words that might fix any of this.

"I don't know what you want from me…" he whispered.

"I don't want anything from you. I want you to leave," Jasper snapped.

Grace stepped between them, her hands raised in a placating gesture. "Jasper, stop. Please."

"No!" Jasper shook his head violently. "He needs to go. She doesn't need this. Neither of them do."

The words devastated Elliot. Was Jasper right? Would Paige and their baby be better off without him?

"I'm not leaving," Elliot forced out. His voice trembled, but the words were iron in his throat. "I love Paige. I am not going to fuck up again."

"Jasper, take a walk," Grace said firmly now, her tone carrying a warning. "Calm down before you do something you regret."

"No, Grace!" Jasper roared. His eyes flicked to his twin, pleading and furious all at once. "Why are you defending him? You've hated him as much as I have since he left."

Grace faltered. Her chin trembled as she spoke from the heart. "I do hate him. I think he's selfish. I think he's a spineless asshole." She glanced at Elliot, her words hitting him like blows. "But Paige needs him. And so does that baby."

The trio fell into a fragile silence, broken only by Elliot's laboured breathing.

Jasper's jaw clenched. His chest rose and fell in ragged heaves. "They're better off without him," he said finally, his voice like steel.

Elliot flinched as though struck again.

Jasper took a step forward, his voice dropping. "Leave now. And if you ever show your face again, I'll kill you myself."

The calm in his tone was more frightening than the earlier rage. Grace instinctively stepped back, her hand half-raised toward her brother, fear flickering in her eyes.

Elliot stood rooted to the spot, every nerve screaming. Dried blood painted his shirt, causing it to stick to his chest. Was he about to run again? Was history about to repeat itself?

Or was this the moment he finally proved he could stay?

CHAPTER TWENTY FIVE

Dear little love,

I found a book of poems on motherhood today and as I read it I felt a mix of so many emotions - excitement, anxiety, fear. You name it I felt it.

It's the same way I felt when I was putting some of your books on the shelf. Some are from when I was little, others I bought just for you.

I can't wait to read you 'Guess How Much I Love You' - that one was always a favourite of mine. Your grandmother bought you 'Love You Forever' and I don't have it in me to read it as an adult.

I remember watching my mother read it to me and the twins, and how she would cry as she got to the end of the story. I always thought it was a nice book, but I didn't quite get it. Now that I have you, I do.

Love,

Mumma

Elliot stumbled up the hospital stairs, each step dragging like lead. The rag pressed to his nose was soaked through, blood dripping warm between his fingers. His head pounded, his vision blurred. He tried in vain to slow the bleeding, but the harder he pressed, the more it smeared.

The stairwell was quiet except for his laboured breaths and the hollow step of his boots on concrete. The walls seemed to close in, sterile white and flickering with the dull hum of fluorescent lights. His mind spun with a million thoughts, each louder than the last. Should he stay? Should he leave? All he seemed capable of was bringing pain to Paige's life. How could he ignore that?

"Don't leave."

The voice echoed behind him, soft but certain.

He turned slowly, blinking through the blur, to find Grace climbing towards him. Her gaze was fixed, holding him in place like a pin through glass. His confusion must have shown, because she pushed forward, her voice sharper.

"If you leave again, she'll never forgive you," she said firmly. "You'll never see your daughter. You'll never have the life we both know you want. And you'll have let your demons win. Again."

He let out a bitter laugh, shaking his head, eyes falling to the steps. "All I do is hurt her. You heard Jasper. He's right. I should just go."

Grace reached the landing, meeting him eye to eye. "Don't listen to him. It doesn't just hurt her, Elliot. It hurts all of us. Jasper's just the one brave enough to say it out loud."

Her voice softened. She hesitated. "I mean… I almost lost my sister because of you."

His head snapped up, his stomach clenching. His voice caught. "What do you mean, you almost lost her?"

"She tried to end her life, Elliot."

The words gutted him, clean and merciless. The air left his lungs. His knees gave way and he collapsed onto the step, legs folding beneath him. The rag slipped from his hand, leaving smudges of red across the concrete.

"What… what?" he stammered, his voice high, broken. "Why?"

Grace slowly sank down next to him, leaning her back against the cold wall. She drew her knees close to her chest, desperate for anything that might make her feel steadier.

"Mum found her on the balcony," she whispered. "She looked like she was about to jump."

Elliot's vision swam and his chest heaved violently, his breath coming in short, ragged bursts. He could see it; could picture it vividly. Paige barefoot on the balcony ledge, wind tugging at her hair, her face streaked with tears. His heart lurched.

"When?" He needed to know.

"The day she found out you got married."

Horror spread through him as the words turned his blood to ice. His eyes widened as the last few months played back in his mind like a cruel film reel - Paige's silence, the unanswered messages, the way she had vanished into herself. He had thought she was angry, but had never suspected she was dying inside.

Grace pressed her forehead to her knees, her voice shaking. "Mum called me, screaming. We didn't know what was happening and Jasper was so upset he punched holes in the wall. We waited for over an hour for someone, anyone, to tell us she was safe."

Her voice cracked, and she choked on a sob.

"You weren't just her world, Elliot. You were ours too. When you left, we lost you… and then we nearly lost her."

The tears came fast and were unstoppable. Spilling for the fear she had buried, the memory of that night and for the pain none of them had known how to heal, Grace cried for her sister, for herself and for the family that had cracked in two.

Elliot sat beside her, stunned beyond reason and unable to find words. Finally - finally - he began to understand the magnitude of what he had done.

"I don't even know what happened," he whispered, his voice raw. He rubbed at his broken nose despite the sting, blood still caked along his lips. "I was drunk in Vegas with Shaun, and the next thing I know, I wake up with a killer hangover… and a wife. I don't love her. I asked her for a divorce, and she threatened to go after custody of the baby if I tried."

He let out a humourless laugh, wiping at his face with the ruined rag. "I don't know what to do."

Grace sniffed, wiping her eyes with the back of her sleeve. "She can't get custody. She has no biological link to the baby. That won't hold up."

"I don't know that for sure. We're married and she could spin it like some twisted surrogate arrangement. Paige doesn't need more battles." His voice broke at the end. "I just want her gone."

"So what are you going to do about it?"

"I don't know. I feel so fucking lost."

"You can't get an annulment if the marriage was consummated," Grace informed him.

He stopped cold, turning to look at Grace. "Actually… I might still qualify."

Her brows drew together. "Wait. You mean you didn't…?"

"Couldn't." His face flushed as he dropped his gaze. "She's tried. A few times. But I just… can't."

Grace blinked in disbelief. "You mean you couldn't have sex with the blonde bimbo you married in Vegas?"

A sharp breath of laughter escaped him despite the shame. He sighed, "No."

Clapping a hand over her mouth, Grace tried in vain to halt the laughter bubbling inside her, but it broke though anyway, spilling out into the stairwell.

"But why?" she asked between giggles.

He tilted his head back, staring at the buzzing light overhead. "Because every time she touched me, I felt nothing but resentment. I couldn't even pretend. All I wanted to do was scream at her and walk out the door." He ran his blood-stained hands through his hair. "She used me. She belittled me. I tried to be the guy who made her happy, gave her everything, but nothing was enough. All it did was make me hate her. And myself."

Grace's laughter softened into sympathy, her smile fading. "I get it. Sorry for laughing."

Elliot shook his head. "No, it's okay. Honestly, it's kind of ridiculous."

Pushing himself to his feet, he swayed for a moment on unsteady legs before offering Grace his hand.

She took it, and he pulled her up.

"I'm going back to Paige," he said, his voice iron-strong. "I need to talk to her."

"Good." Grace wiped the last of her tears. "I'm gonna get food. All this crying is making me hungry."

They parted ways with a shared look of understanding, the kind that didn't need words. For the first time in a long time, Elliot felt like he was walking towards something real.

CHAPTER TWENTY SIX

Framed in the doorway of Paige's hospital room, Elliot was silent. For a long moment he just watched her, the turmoil of the day fading as he drank her in, absorbing the precious sight of her. She lay stroking her swollen belly, her lips moving softly, whispering to the life between them.

"What do you think? Are you a Bailey? Hmm, maybe Olivia? No, that's not quite right. Eliza? Nope…"

She smiled faintly at her own musings, so engrossed in the tempo of naming that she didn't notice him. Elliot's chest thumped. The ritual was intimate, sacred, and for a flicker of a second he felt like an intruder, like he hadn't earned the right to witness it.

"How about Hazel?" he offered gently.

Paige jumped, startled, before letting out a breath. Her mouth tugged into a small smile. "Hmm, no. I don't like that one and apparently, neither does she." She rubbed her ribs where a little foot had just jabbed her.

Elliot chuckled softly and crossed the room. He sat beside her, sliding his hand over the swell of her bump. The warmth of her skin seeped into him, bounding them together. When the baby's foot pressed against his palm, his heart almost broke with wonder. He still couldn't believe they had made this little miracle together.

"What about Ivy?" Paige asked.

She didn't mention what had happened earlier. Not Lexus, not the fight, not even acknowledging the very broken nose before her. For now, she wanted this tiny bubble where nothing else could reach them. Just the three of them.

Elliot, his face freshly washed though mottled with bruises, stayed silent too. He wasn't ready; not yet. This felt safer. This felt real.

"Ivy's nice," he murmured. "What about Violet?"

"Not bad, but still not the one, though."

Every kick sent Paige's heart fluttering. She had longed for this, and now that it was here, Elliot by her side, their daughter moving between them, it felt even more special than she had imagined.

"Eloise?" Elliot offered.

Paige wrinkled her nose dramatically, then brightened as if a lightbulb had gone off. "How about Charlotte?"

She looked at him, hope shimmering in her tired eyes. Elliot stared at her, his gaze softening, mentally tracing the sun-kissed freckles across her nose that he lovingly called her sun kisses; the pink flush of her cheeks; the way her brown hair curled against the pillow.

"Charlotte," he repeated slowly, letting the name settle on his tongue. "Charlotte it is."

They sat in silence for a while, letting the name fill the space between them. Paige stroked her belly, whispering the syllables as if trying them on for size.

Then she said her daughter's name in full: "Charlotte Lawson."

Elliot's head snapped towards her. Once again, his heart hammered in his chest. "Lawson? Wouldn't it be De Luca?"

"No," Paige replied evenly, though her arms folded protectively across her stomach. "I want her to have my last name."

His brows drew together, trying to understand her logic. "But she's my daughter. She should have her father's name."

"She is your daughter," Paige said firmly. "But this is what I want."

"What the hell, Paige? Why?" His voice was louder than he intended, his frustration bleeding into anger. Deep down, he knew it wasn't about the name, it was about what it represented. And in that instant, it felt like she was shutting him out - again.

"Because you left us," she said, her voice trembling but unflinching. "Because I'm the one who's been here. You can't disappear for months and then waltz back in expecting to lay claim."

"I'm not laying claim," Elliot shot back. His hands flexed uselessly at his sides, his chest heaving. "I'm trying to be here now to do right by her. By you."

The air between them grew taut. Elliot jumped to his feet, pacing the small space, while Paige sat straighter in the bed, her arms wrapped tight across her belly as though bracing against more than contractions.

"I'm not trying to punish you, Elliot, honestly I'm not," she added, her voice cracking. "But this, her name, it matters to me. After everything that's happened these past few months, I deserve that."

Her eyes glistened with unshed tears. Elliot turned away from her, running a hand over his bruised jaw, his chest burning with words he couldn't say.

This wasn't just about a name. It was about belonging. Trust.

In the corridor outside Paige's room stood Liam, his hand resting lightly on the handle. He was telling himself he was there for medical reasons - monitoring and readiness - but as he listened to their voices rise and fall, something twisted in his chest, something he couldn't rationalise away. They weren't talking like broken strangers. They were talking like lovers with unfinished business. How that burned him!.

He had seen Paige at her lowest. He had walked her through scans, held her hand when she cried and provided comfort again and again. He had been the steady one. Now Elliot was back, storming in with bruises and apologies, reigniting old flames and opening old flames, as if nothing had happened.

The thought made Liam's jaw clench. What could he do?

Taking a deep breath to compose himself, he knocked once and pushed the door open, wheeling the ultrasound machine inside.

"How are we all doing?" he asked lightly, though he couldn't quite mask his amusement at the tension in the air.

"Fine," Paige and Elliot said in unison, their eyes darting anywhere but each other's.

"Well then," Liam continued smoothly, "time to check on little miss and see how her kidneys are holding up."

He moved toward the chair at Paige's side, the one Elliot had been sitting in moments before, and lowered himself into it with practiced ease. As he prepped the equipment, he caught her gaze for a heartbeat. Even exhausted, even after everything, she carried herself with a quiet dignity that stirred something in him.

Elliot crossed to the other side of the bed, his frown tight. "Why do you keep checking her kidneys?"

Liam ignored him, keeping his tone soft as he looked at Paige. "You ready?"

"Yep," she replied curtly, her voice clipped, the argument over names still bothering her. Without a word, she lifted her gown, baring her bump.

Elliot had seen scans before, but the novelty of them still excited him. Sitting as close as he could, his hand brushed the mattress for balance as if proximity alone could anchor him.

The cool gel made Paige flinch. As the coolness crept across her tummy she relaxed back into the pillow. Liam pressed the transducer gently and the screen flickered to life.

"Hi, baby," Paige whispered, her voice softer now. The wave of love that always consumed her in these moments dominated her expression, easing some of the fury from before.

Elliot's uneven breath also revealed his emotions. Watching the fuzzy image of their daughter as she stretched her limbs, tiny feet kicking, a hand folded close to her face, was nothing short of a miracle. A blessing in black and white.

After a few measured seconds, Liam creased his brow.

"Her kidneys still aren't improving, but the good news is she's measuring at a healthy weight. That might reduce the amount of special care she'll need once she's born."

He smiled supportively at Paige, not even registering Elliot in the room.

"What's wrong with her kidneys?" Elliot asked, his voice rough.

Paige turned, frowning. "What?"

"You've been talking about her kidneys this whole time," he pressed, his voice sharper. "What's wrong with them?"

"Oh, right," Liam said, his tone suddenly cold. "I forgot. You weren't around for any of those appointments."

The words cut like glass. Paige stiffened.

"Liam…" she started, but faltered.

It wasn't professional, she knew it, but he wasn't wrong. Elliot had missed it all - the fear, the tests, the nights she'd lain awake wondering if her baby would be okay.

"She has hydronephrosis," Paige explained quietly, trying to keep her tone an even keel. "It means fluid is building in her kidneys, making them swell."

Elliot's eyes widened. "Is she okay? Is she in pain?"

"At this stage, we don't know," Liam replied, his hostility softening at the raw fear in Elliot's voice. "Her kidneys are enlarged enough that we're concerned she might need surgery after birth, however we won't know for certain until she's here when we'll scan her directly and assess the severity."

The shift in the room was unobtrusive. Despite his misgivings, Liam stopped seeing Elliot as the villain and saw him for what he was in this moment: a terrified father staring down the unknown.

"She might need surgery?" Elliot echoed, his voice empty.

He sank into the chair at Paige's side, his eyes fixed on the screen. Reaching for his hand instinctively to offer some comfort, Paige's gesture was rebuffed. Elliot pulled away, drawing inwards instead.

"Why didn't you tell me?" His voice splintered, accusation cutting through the fear.

"I tried," Paige said quickly. "I called you the day we found out but you didn't pick up. You never called back."

"And today?" His eyes flicked to hers, sharp. "Why didn't you tell me today?"

Paige blinked, caught. "Elliot, we've had a lot to talk about. I just… I didn't know how to bring it up."

"Were you hiding it from me?" panic manifested sharply into anger.

"What? No! Why would I hide something like that?" Her voice lifted too, defensive, her cheeks flushing with hurt.

"For fuck's sake… " Elliot buried his face in his hands, dragging them down over his mouth as he tried to remember to breathe. This was too much - the diagnosis, the guilt, the what-ifs - all piling up until he thought he might crack.

Liam cleared his throat, stepping carefully into the chasm. "I'm going to get one of our social workers to talk with you both. There's a lot going on. It might help to start sorting through this before the baby arrives."

Neither answered. The silence between Paige and Elliot was deafening, weighted with years of love and disappointment.

Liam pushed the ultrasound machine aside and stood. His chest constricted as he glanced at Paige once more. He shouldn't be feeling this way. He knew it. And yet, deep down, he was.

He wanted her.

It was this wanting her that was clouding everything.

Stepping out into the corridor, guilt pressed down on him like a lead weight. The muffled sounds of machines hummed behind the closed door. He let out a breath he hadn't realised he'd been holding.

That room was no place for a child. Not yet.

CHAPTER TWENTY SEVEN

Dear little love,

Everything feels too loud - from things outside my window to the blood coursing through my veins.

The world keeps spinning like nothing's changed but that's a false positive. I can hear cars, laughter, music... and I just want to scream at it to stop.

You're the only thing that keeps me tethered. When you kick, the noise fades for a second. It's like you're saying, stay with me.

Love,

Mumma

Theresa

"I don't know what to do, Rosa," Theresa shared softly, cradling her coffee like a lifeline. The styrofoam cup had gone lukewarm in her hands, but she held it anyway, seeking comfort in the faint heat. Her body sagged against the plastic chair, the gravity of the last few days leaving her exhausted to the marrow.

"Neither do I," Rosa admitted.

Their friendship had become a strange comfort over the past months. Built on the debris of their children's crumbling relationship, it was now their vital port during a medical storm. She reached for Theresa's free hand, squeezing it. Two women, bound not by blood, but by their shared love for a little girl who hadn't yet taken her first breath.

The muted sounds of hospital life - footsteps squeaking on linoleum, the faint beep of monitors through thin walls, the occasional muffled cough - was the background to their existence these days. The women spent every waking hour on the ward; the easy silence between them overlaid with overpowering concern and love for their first grandchild.

Inside the room, a different sort of silence reigned.

Elliot

Lying back against the pillow, Paige's gaze was fixed on the ceiling tiles as if they held the answers she couldn't find in herself. Her throat burned, but tears no longer fell. Her body ached, her belly taut with both life and fear while her heart… her heart was in pieces.

Paige rebuked herself. If only she had kept her distance all those years ago when Elliot first introduced himself. If only she had simply smiled politely instead of falling headlong into his mesmerising green eyes. If only she knew then, what she knew how… she would not be here, torn between love and loathing, her chest aching with regrets.

Elliot sat beside her, hunched forward, his head buried in his hands. His thoughts battered him like waves, one crashing harder than the next.

Anger. Fear. Frustration. Guilt.

And beneath them all, love.

It roared inside him so loud it was suffocating. He loved Paige; God how he loved her! And how he loved his unborn daughter too! The tragedy was he'd promised her forever, but forever doesn't survive a lie.

The wound he'd caused lay open between them. Every unanswered call. Every lie he'd believed. Every night she'd cried alone. Each time Paige refused to meet his eyes it gutted him, reminding him that this could be his last chance to put things right.

Hydronephrosis. The word rattled around his head like a curse. He didn't even know how to spell it, but the sound alone made him nauseous. It was a shadow hanging over the future, a threat to the tiny miracle kicking beneath Paige's ribs.

The anger in his chest coiled tighter - anger at Shaun, at Lexus, at himself. He wanted to hold Paige and tell her they would face the future together; swear he would never leave again. How could he do that if she wouldn't even look at him?

By the time he lifted his head, night had fallen. The city outside glowed in neon and headlights, but this room felt detached, like a bubble floating above the world. Just the two of them. Three, if he let himself hope.

He couldn't waste this.

"Paige?" His voice cracked, hoarse and broken.

She turned her head at last, a single tear visible on her cheek.

"Elliot."

He looked wrecked. The man she had loved was still in there, buried under months of manipulation and bad decisions, and the sight of him made her chest ache even as her mind screamed at her to detach.

"I don't know what to do," he whispered.

"Neither do I."

"We're going to be parents in a few hours."

"I noticed," she murmured, dry and biting. Sarcasm was her armour. It always had been. He didn't flinch; he knew better than to take it personally.

"What do you want?" His eyes pleaded. He wasn't referring to baby names; he was asking for his life back.

"I don't know," she answered, her voice giving away her anxiety and fears.

"I know you've got something going on with that doctor," he said quietly, almost ashamed of the words.

Her head snapped toward him. "What? No. Why would you say that?"

"You don't have to lie. It's okay. I can see he cares about you and that you seem to care back."

She hesitated, then exhaled. "There's nothing going on."

"Paige..." His voice held both doubt and resignation.

Her shoulders slumped. "Okay. We kissed. That's all. We're not together but… there's something." Her voice faltered, weighted with shame.

The words gutted him, twisting his stomach into knots. Nodding slowly, jaw tightening, he forced himself to ask the questions that scared him most of all.

"Do you love him?"

She froze, the question throwing her off balance. Did she love Liam? No. Not like that. Not yet. She liked him, yes; a lot, maybe, but love?

"I… I don't know."

"Do you want him to be Charlotte's father?"

The question slapped her harder than any insult. Rocked to her core, the answer came fast: "No. No, I don't."

The simple truth was that it had always been Elliot. No one else had ever touched her soul the same way.

"So what do you want, Paige?" he asked again, gentler this time.

"What do you mean?"

"Whatever you want, I'll do it. If you want me to step away so you can be with him, I'll do it. If you want to co-parent, I'll do that too. And if you want us, really want us… I'm all in. Just say it."

Elliot laid bare his feelings, caught between hope and dread. He had finally shared everything with her and his entire world - their world - hinged on her reply.

"I meant it when I said I love you, Paige. I've hurt you - I know that. I've been weak. I may not be worthy of you but I need you to know you're the love of my life, the only woman I have ever loved."

Paige met his gaze, truly believing that he had spoken what was in his heart. As she looked at the green eyes that had once made her feel like she was the centre of his universe, her heart squeezed. Words rose to her lips and died there, her fear louder than their mutual love.

"I… I don't know," she whispered. After what seemed like an eternity, she reciprocated and asked him the same question.

"What do you want?"

"I want you," he said, his voice shaking but certain. "I want a life with you; with our daughter. I want Sunday dinners at your mum's house, where Grace complains about the food and Jasper cheats at board games. I want to teach her how to ride a bike and take her to see the ocean for the first time. I want to sit beside you on the porch thirty years from now, grey hair and all, and still feel the same way I do when you look at me now."

His words tumbled out quickly. They had been bottled up for months and there was no restraining them any longer.

"I want our mornings back, when you'd steal the blanket and pretend not to hear me complaining, and I'd let you, because you'd smile in your sleep. I want to read our daughter your books, to show her the worlds you've built, to tell her her mum is the cleverest, bravest, strongest woman I've ever known. I want to make up for every moment I missed; every tear I caused. I want to prove that I'm not the man who left you; that I am the man who stayed."

He swallowed hard, his eyes burning.

"I want forever with you, Paige. Nothing less."

His outpouring of love overwhelmed her. As much as she wanted to reach for him and melt into his arms, the familiar ache in her chest reminded her that it would be foolish to rush into any decision. Her recent heartbreaks had left indelible scars on her psyche, scars which were still to fully heal. She needed time to trust herself before she could commit to trusting him forever.

"I need time to think, Elio," she answered finally.

He nodded once, his face shadowed with pain. He stood, walking towards the door with laboured steps that mirrored his weighted heart. At the threshold, he turned back.

"No matter what you choose, even if it's for me to walk away, please know that I love you. And I'm sorry," he said gently.

The door clicked shut behind him.

Paige let out a breath she hadn't realised she was holding. Before she could gather herself, the door opened again.

Liam stepped in, his expression unreadable. His eyes flicked briefly to where Elliot had stood moments earlier, then landed on Paige with something softer, heavier.

CHAPTER TWENTY EIGHT

Dear little love,

I wish your father were here, but he isn't. It's just us.

Just us.

Love,

Mumma

Paige

Liam watched Paige lie motionless on the bed, unsure what to say. The silence seemed interminable.

"I think we should talk," he said finally. "I want to apologise for how I acted before. It wasn't fair to you or Elliot."

She remained quiet, waiting.

"I told you I wanted to protect you," he continued. "And I meant that, but the truth is I feel like I've been fighting for someone just out of reach."

She nodded slightly, struggling to soak up the meaning behind his words while her brain fought to catch up with the events of the last twenty four hours.

"What do you want, Liam?" she asked. "Once this baby's here, I'm not your patient anymore."

"I know," he said, moving a step closer. "If I'm honest, that terrifies me. For months, you've been the highlight of my week. I looked forward to our appointments, hoping they'd run long. I'd catch myself scanning the halls, hoping to see your smile… that smile that just takes the air out of my lungs."

Her cheeks flushed. "Really?"

"Yes," he said, his voice thick with emotion. "I know we've only known each other a few months, but I need to show you what it's like to be really loved; to be appreciated."

Her breath caught in her throat. The words were beautiful. Too beautiful.

"I think about you constantly. About you and the baby. I wonder what it would feel like… to hold her, to hold you. You awoke something in me I thought was long dead."

"My job wasn't to fix you, Liam."

"I know that. And I'm not saying that's what you are to me. You're more than that."

She swallowed hard, but didn't speak.

"I'm going to be blunt because I don't want to regret not saying this. I'm not in love with you yet, but I can feel myself heading that way and I'd really like to explore whatever is happening between us."

Her chest tightened, crushing under the emotional strain of this moment. She wasn't ready for this - for any of this.

"You don't have to say anything," Liam added quickly, misreading the silence. "I just needed you to know."

He stepped closer, slowly leaning in, eyes fixed on her lips.

She turned her face sharply so his kiss landed awkwardly on her cheek.

The heat of shame climbed her neck as he pulled back. Neither spoke.

A moment later, the door closed behind him, leaving her alone with her jumbled thoughts.

Sinking into the pillow, pulling the sheet up around her shoulders, there was only one thing going through her mind.

What the hell is happening to my life.

CHAPTER TWENTY NINE

Paige groaned. Her chest ached, her stomach churned. How had she gotten herself into this mess? Was this really what she wanted or needed?

Threading her fingers through her hair, she gave herself permission to imagine a different future. A future with Liam. On paper it made perfect sense. He was stable, dependable and already a father.

The image cracked as soon as added herself to the picture. Dropping into a ready-made family with two little humans to care for when she could barely keep her own head above water, petrified her. The thought nearly suffocated her, compounding every fear she had ever had about her ability to be a mother. A good mother. A mother her daughter had every right to have.

As the familiar prickle of tears crept in, she was startled by a voice tender with concern.

"Are you okay?"

She hadn't heard her sister enter, consumed as she was by the carousel of events that day.

"Yeah," Paige answered quickly, too quickly, giving her away.

"Liar," Grace said gently, shaking her head.

"I'm sorry…"

"Stop. Stop apologising. Just talk to me."

She reached out and took Paige's hand, careful to avoid the needle bruise at the back of it. Paige stared at the connection for a long time, then exhaled.

"I just don't know what to do," she whispered, the admission loosening something tight in her chest.

"About what exactly?"

"About… everything."

Muddled words rushed out before she had time to put them into some sort of order.

"Am I ready to be a mum? It's happening today, in a few hours, whether I think I am or not. Am I doing her a disservice by keeping her?"

Her own voice startled her. She had wrestled with doubts before - about whether she'd be good enough or strong enough - but never once had the possibility of not keeping her baby formed in her mind. Now, here it was, falling out of her mouth and she couldn't take it back.

"What are you talking about?" Grace asked, alarm flashing across her face.

The writer in Paige paused, trying to articulate her doubts as best she could.

"Elliot and I are a mess. I know he could be a good father, but he's broken, and that won't help her. And me? I'm no better. A few weeks ago I had a breakdown, just because he'd married someone else. What kind of mother does that, especially while pregnant?"

Her words tumbled faster, spinning out of control.

"How could I do that to her? Why would I even think about it? And now he's back saying he wants to make it right, but how can I trust him? He left me for someone else, then married a stranger and told me the baby wasn't his. Then there's Liam... I don't even know if I actually like him or if I just needed to feel wanted. Plus he can be so cruel sometimes! Not to me, but to Elliot. I mean, what does it say about a man who can be cruel to the man I once loved and about me for even considering a relationship with him?"

Her chest rose and fell in sharp bursts.

"Let's not forget that he's my doctor too! What kind of idiot hooks up with their doctor? And how can I be sure he's not doing this on a regular basis?"

She collapsed back against the pillow, drained, her breath ragged.

When she was spent, Grace continued to hold her sister's hand and leaned closer until her face was just inches away from hers.

"Paige... breathe. Just breathe. Everything is going to be alright."

"How do you know that?" Paige demanded, fresh tears clinging to her lashes. "How could you possibly know that?"

"Because I know you," Grace answered simply. Her voice trembled, but her eyes stayed steady.

"You've been protecting people your whole life. You looked after me and Jasper when Mum was working double shifts. You made us dinner when you were barely old enough to use the stove. You sat with Jasper all night when he had the flu because he only wanted you there. And when I got picked on at school, you didn't think twice about stepping in in front of me, even when it meant you took the hit instead. That's who you are, Paige. You put yourself between the people you love and the things that hurt them."

She looked at her sister with unbridled affection and continued.

"Do you really think that kind of person won't be a good mum? Paige, you've been practising for this your whole life. Your daughter will be the luckiest little girl in the world.

Paige felt the load on her shoulders lift slightly at her sister's words. But Grace wasn't finished yet.

"If you choose Elliot, I'll support you. If you choose Liam, I'll support you. If you choose adoption, I'll support you. Whatever you need, I'll fight for you, more so when you feel like you can't fight for yourself," she promised.

"What you need to remember, Paige, is that you don't have to do it alone. Mum, Jasper and I… we've got your back. That means midnight phone calls, showing up when you're tired and don't think you can do another feed, stepping in when you need to scream into a pillow and just breathe. Always. You're not in this by yourself, Paige. You never were.

"I just don't think you realise how amazing you are. You don't see yourself the way we do but, I promise you, when you hold that baby in your arms, she'll see it. She'll see you. All of you. The same woman who's been saving people her whole life."

The words washed over Paige like a balm. Her breathing slowed, her pulse easing its frantic drum. Tears still slipped down her cheeks, but now they carried gratitude, not despair.

"Thank you," she whispered hoarsely. "I just… I don't know what to do."

As if summoned by her confession, a soft knock came at the door.

Both sisters turned. A red-haired woman with kind eyes stepped inside, holding a notepad against her chest.

"Hi, I hope I'm not interrupting. I'm Leslie, one of the social workers here. Dr Baker asked me to stop by. Is now a good time?"

Paige froze, her throat closing. A social worker. Suddenly, her doubts felt dangerous, official, like saying them aloud could change everything. She hesitated, then gave the smallest nod.

Grace bent and pressed a kiss to her sister's forehead. "I'll be right outside," she pledged, before slipping past Leslie and closing the door behind her.

Leslie took the chair Grace had left, setting her notepad down gently. She leaned forward, her tone warm and patient.

"So Paige, tell me what's been going on. How can I help?"

Paige stared at her, chest rising and falling in shallow breaths. She opened her mouth once, closed it, and then opened it a second time, forcing herself to speak.

"Umm... lots. I... I want to know about..." Her throat caught, the word thick with fear.

"About adoption."

CHAPTER THIRTY

Dear little love,

I need you to know something in case I can't say it later — I never stopped fighting for you. Even when I was too scared to move, I was still fighting in quiet ways.

I don't know if I've been brave or just foolish, but I'd do it all again to have you.

Love,

Mumma

Elliot

Elliot sat slumped outside Paige's hospital room, his head buried in his hands. Shame, his constant buddy these days, rolled off him in waves, each breath a rasp of guilt. Rosa sat close, her hand on his shoulder.

"Mum, please," he whispered hoarsely. "Just stop."

"No, figlio mio. You need to fight for her. Fight for your family."

"I am fighting!" His voice cracked, raw and wild. "I told her I love her. I told her I'll take whatever she gives me, whether that's a second chance or just co-parenting. I'm not going to chain her to me like a prisoner."

He stared at his hands, skin dry and raw from stress. His career had stalled, his bank account was being bled dry by his wife's greed and his pride was shredded to ribbons.

Right on cue, like a demon summoned from the pits of hell, her voice reverberated down the corridor.

"Well, well, well! Look what we have here."

Lexus swayed toward him, her hips moving from side to side like she was strutting a runway. Shaun swaggered at her side, a triumphant smirk plastered across his face.

Elliot's head snapped up. A low growl rumbled from deep within as he surged to his feet. Behind him, Theresa, Grace, Jasper and Rosa scrambled up in alarm.

"What the hell are you doing here?" Elliot demanded, voice sharp enough to cut glass.

"I came to get my husband," Lexus purred, tossing her blonde hair, her acrid perfume following in her wake.

"And I came to rescue my idiot best friend," Shaun added with a grin. "Come on, Prince. Go home to your wife."

"No." Elliot's voice was on fire. "You two need to leave. Now."

"I'm not leaving until our baby is born," Lexus sang sweetly, her smile a razor blade in lipstick.

"My baby. Not yours," Elliot hissed.

"Nah, Prince. I'm pretty sure it's hers," Shaun chuckled darkly.

Elliot's eyes snapped to him, blazing. "Don't you dare..."

Shaun leaned in close, his voice oily. "What? Did I dream up that story about Paige being your surrogate? Or was that one of your lies, too?"

The red mist came before Elliot even realised he'd moved. His fist connected with Shaun's jaw - bone on bone - the crack resounding along the corridor. Shaun slammed into the wall with a grunt. Gasps ripped through the waiting area, nurses shouting, Grace's hands flying to her mouth.

"She is my daughter!" Elliot roared, lunging forward.

"If either of you so much as breathe near her or Paige, I swear to God I will kill you both!"

Shaun straightened slowly, blood dripping from his split lip. And then he laughed.

"You hear that, Lex?" he crooned, spitting red onto the floor. "Prince thinks he's still the hero."

"Not for long," Lexus sneered.

Shaun launched. His shoulder barrelled into Elliot's chest, sending them both crashing to the linoleum. Fists rained down on Elliot's face, reopening old bruises, new blood splattering. Rosa screamed. Theresa shouted for help. Jasper lunged, only for security to thunder in and haul Shaun off, Liam storming behind them, fury written across his face.

"This is a hospital, for Christ's sake!" Liam roared.

"He started it!" Elliot spat, his nose bent grotesquely. "Screaming about my kid..."

"Your kid?" Liam's voice was venomous. "Please. She might have your DNA, but you're no father. You're nothing."

"Fuck you! She's my daughter!" Elliot howled, his voice shredded, chest heaving.

"Oh, give it a rest," Jasper snapped. "You're a piss-weak excuse for a father."

"Shut up, Jasper!" Grace shrieked.

"What? Because I'm telling the truth?"

"Enough!" Theresa screamed, her face red with fury.

"Don't you yell at my son!" Rosa shot back, her voice shaking the walls.

"I am her father!" Elliot bellowed, staggering to his feet, his face streaming blood. His chest heaved, desperation clawing through his words.

"If you're the father, then that makes me the mother," Lexus cut in smugly, crossing her arms.

"NO!" the entire group roared in unison.

Lexus flashed her arrogant grin. "What? Just stating the facts."

"You need to back off, De Luca," Liam growled, stepping in front of Elliot. "Let Paige be happy for once."

"Why? So you can slide into her bed?" Elliot spat, eyes wild. "You think you're her knight in shining armour? You're just a vulture circling her pain."

"I'd do a better job loving her than you ever did," Liam snapped back.

"You're just a fucked-up doctor with a thing for screwing patients," Grace hit out.

Rosa gasped, scandalised. "You're sleeping with Paige?"

"No!" Liam snapped, then softer, more dangerous: "But I love her."

Theresa barked a bitter laugh. "You call that love? You took advantage of an emotionally vulnerable woman in the throes of a breakdown after knowing her for a whole five minutes. That's not love, that's grooming."

"I'm not using her," Liam shot back, fire in his eyes. "I love your daughter. We're going to be together."

"Over my dead body," Jasper growled.

"She doesn't love you," Liam snapped, his chest rising and falling. "I know she has feelings for me."

"She loves me," Elliot rasped, his face a mask of blood and desperation. "She always has."

A small crowd had gathered now, nurses and patients whispering furiously. Phones lifted. And then, of course, Shaun opened his mouth.

"Are you kidding me?" he barked a laugh. "Paige Lawson screwing her doctor? This'll be on the front page by morning!"

CRACK.

Liam's fist connected with Shaun's nose with brutal precision, dropping him to the floor. Shaun writhed, groaning, blood pooling fast.

Liam crouched low, his voice a scalpel. "If you ever go near her again, I'll make sure you can't walk. I know anatomy, Shaun. I know how to break you in ways no one else will see."

For once, Shaun's confidence faltered. He stumbled, backing away, blood dripping. Lexus scowled, flipped her hair, and followed him out with a huff.

Breathing raggedly, Liam turned back. His eyes scanned Elliot's battered face, his voice low and final.

"I told Paige how I feel and I know she's going to choose me. Right now, though, my only concern is getting that baby here safely, so back off, or so help me, I'll make sure you're out of her life for good."

And then it came.

A scream.

Piercing. Gut-wrenching.

Every head whipped towards Paige's room.

Without a word, the group bolted. Grace shoved the door open, her heart in her throat.

Inside, Paige writhed on the bed, doubled over, her face contorted in agony.

Her voice was a gasp, broken and raw.

"It's happening. She's coming. NOW!"

CHAPTER THIRTY ONE

Dear little love,
Everything hurts. Everything feels too much.
I love you.
Love,
Mumma

Paige

Paige talked with the social worker for what felt like hours, though the clock only said forty-five minutes. Long enough to empty her heart and imagine a hundred possible futures, none of which felt like the one. She had the information now, all the answers she thought she wanted, but could she do it? Could she go through with adoption, sign her name on a dotted line and then wake up every morning knowing her daughter was out there without her?

The thought turned over and over in her mind like a broken record.

And then the pain came.

It was sudden, savage, tearing through her abdomen and clawing around to her back until her breath fractured into a scream. It felt like her body had been split open from the inside. Her vision blurred and the room's white walls melted into a swirl of colour as nurses flooded the room.

"Stay with me, Paige. Deep breaths!" someone barked.

The nausea hit next, violent and unrelenting. A nurse thrust a bag in front of her face - just in time - as she vomited, her body convulsing, skin burning as if set alight. Voices blurred together in a chorus of panic.

"I'm just giving you something for the pain..." a calm voice said near her ear.

She turned her head sluggishly. A nurse hovered above her, smiling gently as she injected something into the IV. Behind her, Paige's mother stood rooted to the floor, eyes wide with horror, a trembling hand covering her mouth.

Paige tried to focus on her mum in an effort to centre herself, but the room spun faster. A terrible thought slammed into her chest like a knife.

What if I'm dying?

Her head rolled, eyes darting desperately from face to face. And then the sheets were yanked away.

Gasps exploded through the room.

Her eyes dragged downward, fighting the haze, until she saw it.

A spreading pool of blood, thick and black, staining everything in its wake. Dripping down the bed, the metallic tang filled her nose. The smell of iron and salt set her off again, her stomach lurching on its own journey. She vomited, gagging on bile, even as the edges of her vision dimmed.

"What's happening?!" Elliot's voice shattered through the chaos, raw with terror.

Liam didn't answer him. His jaw was set, his hands firm as he pressed down on her swollen belly, assessing, calculating. His eyes flicked to the monitors, then to the blood, then back to her face.

"Prep the OR!" he snapped, his professional calm fraying at the edges. A nurse darted for the door.

Liam leaned close, his voice steady but his eyes betraying fear.

"Paige, it looks like your placenta has detached from your uterus. We need to get you into surgery immediately for an emergency Caesarean."

The words barely made sense, crashing into her ears like static.

"Will she be okay?" Paige whispered, her throat scraped raw.

"We're going to do everything we can to keep you both safe," Liam said, not answering the question directly, his twitching jaw revealing the extent of his distress.

He glanced towards her mother.

"Do you want her with you, Paige?"

Paige shook her head weakly. Her eyes sought Elliot instead, offering him a shaking hand in invitation.

"Will you... will you...?"

Elliot was at her side instantly, gripping her hand so tightly it hurt.

"Of course. I'm not leaving you."

He pressed his lips to her knuckles, a vow of desperation.

Liam's face darkened as he spotted this exchange, the silent fury unmistakable.

"Fine," Liam bit out. "But we're moving now!"

The nurses descended, wheeling her bed into motion, the room blurring into streaks of white and blue. Elliot jogged alongside, clinging to her hand until a nurse pulled him back with brisk author-ity. "You need to scrub in."

Fluorescent lights flashed overhead as they sped her down the corridor, each one blinding her before darkness swallowed her vision again.

My dear baby, she thought, clinging to the words like a prayer.

If I don't make it out, please remember I love you. I love you more than anything.

And then the world went black.

CHAPTER THIRTY TWO

Before Paige knew it, she was lying in the cold, sanitised operating theatre. The lights above her were blinding, white and merciless, reflecting off silver trays that gleamed with instruments. The sharp scent of antiseptic stung her nose, mixing with the copper tang of her own blood that caked her skin.

The anaesthetist had already administered the spinal, and now she was numb from the chest down. She tested her legs, willing them to move, but nothing happened. A jolt of terror hit her. She was a prisoner in her own body.

She took a wavering breath, her chest rising in shallow bursts as a blue curtain was pulled up across her abdomen, cutting off her view. She swallowed hard. She knew it was there to protect her, but all she could imagine was what lay just beyond it: her skin sliced open, blood spilling, hands tugging her baby into the world.

"All right, Paige," Liam's voice came from behind his mask, clipped but steady. "I'm going to start now. Let me know if you feel anything unusual or get dizzy."

Her voice trembled as she whispered, "But... Elliot isn't here yet."

"Yes, I am."

She turned her head toward the sound and saw him hurrying toward her, scrub cap crooked, blue gown rustling. His eyes, even bruised and bloodshot, softened the moment they landed on her. He bent until his face was level with hers. A single tear slipped down her cheek, and he wiped it away with his thumb, leaving his palm cradling her face.

"This is it," he said, in a soft hush.

They didn't need words after that. The look in his eyes said every-thing - fear, love, regret, devotion. She let herself drown in it because, if this was her last memory, she wanted it to be him.

On the other side of the curtain, Liam's scalpel touched skin. Paige's eyes widened. Elliot's hand applied more pressure in support.

"I feel it," she breathed, voice barely audible.

His whole body jerked. "Does it hurt?"

"No... not pain. Pressure. Tugging." She struggled, her words disjointed. "Like someone's pulling me apart."

Elliot glanced at the nurse, panic rising in his chest. She gave a gentle nod. "That's normal, Dad."

Relief washed over him, but it didn't last.

"Are you okay?" asked, catching the tension in his jaw.

He forced a smile. "Yeah. I'm here - and we're about to meet our little girl."

The forced lie was necessary as he didn't want to upset Paige. Not now. The truth was that there was a storm inside him. He was not okay. The last forty-eight hours had ripped him open: the fights, the shame, the blood. Now, here he was, inches away from losing the only two people who mattered to him. He was teetering on the edge of a cliff, unsure if the ledge would hold.

"No, don't lie to me," Paige murmured, her eyes searching his.

"I'm okay," he repeated, softer this time. It sounded like a prayer more than a truth.

She didn't believe him. She longed to touch his face, but her arms were immovable and lay useless at her sides. Instead she studied him - the dark circles, the scruff of his jaw, the green of his eyes, still daring to hope.

In spite of everything, she felt at peace.

And that peace shattered in an instant.

The alarms began first. A shrill, unrelenting blare. Then came the voices - sharp, urgent, overlapping. Hands moved fast, bodies pressing close. The cadence of the room had changed from careful precision to controlled panic.

Her ears filling with static, Paige saw Elliot's mouth move, unable to hear the words. She wanted to ask what was happening, but her tongue was heavy. Her body floated, light and untethered.

She closed her eyes.

And opened them somewhere else.

She was on a park bench in Central Park. The world was gold and crimson, autumn leaves cascading around her, the air rich with roasted nuts and the organic perfume of damp earth. Sunlight poured through the branches overhead.

"Mummy!"

Her heart stumbled at the sound. She turned.

On the seesaw sat a little girl, bundled in a puffy jacket, dark curls bouncing as she shifted up and down. No older than three, her cheeks were flushed from the crisp air. When she looked up, she saw green eyes. Elliot's eyes.

Paige's chest broke open. Her daughter.

"Do you want some help, Lottie?" she asked, her voice lilting like a melody.

"No, I can do it," Charlotte grunted, fumbling with her buttons.

Paige laughed softly. "Okay, baby."

A moment later the little girl's face crumpled. "Please help?"

Paige knelt and fastened the coat, her fingers trembling with tenderness. "You know something? I love you more than anything in this world."

Charlotte's lips twitched into a grin. "No, I love you more."

Paige's eyes stung. "No, I love you more."

"No, I love you more!" Charlotte shouted, giggling, rubbing her nose against Paige's. Their laughter rang out, bright and endless, filling the playground and nourishing Paige's soul.

She leaned back, memorising it. The sound of her daughter's joy. The curve of her cheeks. The way sunlight turned her curls to gold.

Then the edges blurred. The warmth drained. The laughter thinned until it was gone.

In its place, a single, sharp beep.

Panic washed over her. Desperate to touch her daughter again, Paige reached out, but her arms wouldn't move. The world darkened.

Beep.

Her chest tightened.

Beep.

Elliot's voice pierced through, frantic. "Paige! Stay with me! Don't you dare leave me!"

Beep.

Her eyelids fluttered, heavy as lead. She fought the blackness, wrestling her way back to the present.

Finally her eyes opened.

CHAPTER THIRTY THREE

Dear little love,
No matter what comes next, you are my beginning and my redemption.
Love,
Mumma

The first time Paige opened her eyes, the light above her burned her retinas like a midday sun, forcing her to squeeze them shut again with a soft whimper.

The second time, she heard voices. Soft, hurried chatter, like a dream hovering just out of reach. She drifted along, caught between sleep and waking.

The third time, her eyelids fluttered open and stayed that way. The fog in her head lifted slowly, like a retreating tide. Reality crept back in.

She felt the tug of the pulse oximeter on her finger; the ache of the cannula taped to her hand. She was well aware of the soreness that spread like fire through her arm and abdomen; every nerve screaming and acknowledging her existence.

Her throat rasped as she forced out a single word.

"Charlotte..."

The shadow beside her stirred, forming into her mother's worried face. Theresa's eyes were red from sleeplessness, but they softened instantly. She brushed a hand over Paige's warm forehead, the way she had a million times before.

"It's okay, darling. She's okay."

"Charlotte." She uttered the name again - louder, rougher.

Another figure leaned forward in response. Rosa, the strain of the day visible in every delicate crease around her eyes.

"She's with Elliot," Rosa whispered. "She's alright."

"Take me to her." Paige's voice was scratchy but her resolve was iron.

"Sweetheart, you've just had major surgery. You lost a lot of blood. You've been asleep for a whole day. You need to rest," Theresa pleaded, her hand firm against Paige's shoulder.

"No. I need to see her."

Paige's body screamed in protest as she tried to sit up, excruciating pain tearing through her abdomen. Still, she kept moving, ignoring Theresa and Rosa as they tried to stop her, voices thick with alarm. What they didn't know was that Paige's daughter was imbuing her mother with strength, making her a force to be reckoned with.

Reluctantly accepting they could not stop her, Rosa darted off to fetch a wheelchair. She reappeared a short while later, helping Paige into it with painstaking care. Theresa muttered apologies to the nurses who tried to intervene.

"She isn't stable," one of them snapped. "She needs to lie down."

"If you don't move, I will crawl there myself," Paige growled, her voice low and shaking with fury,

Silence. And then the nurses stepped back.

The wheelchair rolled smoothly down the corridor under Theresa's guidance. The sign for NICU came into view and Paige exhaled a breath she hadn't noticed she was holding. Her heart thudded painfully, each beat whispering the same word.

Closer. Closer.

The heavy doors gave way, releasing her into the gleaming sterility of the NICU. As with every hospital ward in the world, she was first struck by the distinctive smell of antibacterial solution attacking her nostrils. Paige noted a handful of nurses moving with care amongst the small transparent cribs housed in the special care nursery, each incubator a temporary home for a little premature babe. She scanned the room hastily, her throbbing heart in her mouth.

She saw the two figures standing over one incubator: Elliot and Liam.

Her pulse spiked, anger and betrayal searing through her. Both men had contributed to the chaos that was her life but, now was not the time to pay heed to them. She was focussed on one thing only.

"Paige?" Liam stepped forward first, his voice low and commanding. "You shouldn't be up. When did you wake?"

"Are you okay?" Elliot added quickly, his voice raw with worry.

She ignored them both.

Pain lanced through her middle as she forced herself from the chair. Her legs trembled, her stitches pulled, but she took one step. Then another.

And then she saw her.

Inside the incubator, wrapped in blankets that swamped her tiny body, was her baby. Charlotte.

The world stopped spinning.

So impossibly small, her hands were no larger than coins. Her skin was delicate, red and wrinkly, and a dusting of black hair crowned her fragile head. Her lips, pouty and familiar, were all Paige - perfectly formed but in miniature. Despite the nasal cannula, Paige could see it unmistakably - Elliot's nose and his cheekbones. It made her wonder if she'd inherit his rogue little dimple too, the one that surfaced whenever he forgot to guard his smile.

Tears trickled down Paige's face as she pressed a shaking hand against the incubator. Her chest caved in, her breath caught between a sob and a prayer.

Elliot watched Paige meet their daughter for the first time with wonder, pride and immense love. Her body was stitched and broken, her spirit raw, but she looked stronger and more beautiful than he had ever seen her before. Every heartbreak, every betrayal, every wound had led to this single, sacred moment and, as he watched her, he knew with certainty that he would love her until his last breath.

"Would you like to hold her?" a voice asked gently.

Startled, Paige turned around to see a tall man in scrubs had sidled up near them. Incredibly grateful, all she could do was nod wordlessly, awestruck by her little treasure.

With Rosa and Theresa's help, Paige lowered herself into the cushioned chair beside the incubator. Glenn worked with steady hands, gently lifting Charlotte and placing her against her mother's chest.

Liam stepped forward and undid the ties of Paige's gown without asking. She shot him a wary glance. His voice was clipped, professional.

"It's called kangaroo care. Skin to skin helps regulate her temperature and heartbeat."

Paige nodded faintly, though her attention was already on Charlotte.

The moment their bodies touched, something ancient and wild ignited inside her. A warmth surged through her chest, erasing every ounce of fear, every scar of grief. It was just them now. Just mother and daughter.

Charlotte twitched softly, her tiny mouth scrunching into dreams. Her breaths were shallow but steady. Paige bent her head and began to hum a lullaby she hadn't sung since childhood, the melody spilling out as if it had been waiting for this moment.

The world fell away. The NICU, the chaos, the men hovering like shadows. There was only Charlotte. Only love.

Elliot crouched beside them, unable to look away. He had felt it before when Liam lifted their daughter into the world as Paige bled out - the flush of sudden, heart-swelling love of love. It had partnered with terror then, but now, with Paige on the road to recovery, it had grown into an incomparable torrent of mindblowing love - a wave of emotion that swallowed everything else whole.

Paige turned to him, the tears unabating.

"Thank you," she whispered.

Elliot frowned. "For what?"

"For her," Paige said simply. "Thank you for giving me her."

Her bruised hand rose, trembling with IV tape, and cupped his cheek. Elliot closed his eyes, leaning into her touch as his tears spilled freely, joining hers.

This was his family. His heart. His second chance.

And just beyond the circle of light, a shadow burned.

Liam.

He stood back, jaw ticking, fingers curling sharply into his palms. The warmth Paige once drew out of him had curdled into something sharp and bitter. He watched as her hand touched Elliot's cheek, and something inside him snapped.

Without a word, he turned on his heels. His scrubs rustling down the corridor until the cold night swallowed him.

Outside, under the amber streetlamps of the hospital car park, his rage exploded. His fists slammed into brick, again and again, until red streaked his skin and pain lit fire through his arms.

"How could you let this happen again?" His voice broke against the stone. He stared at the blood dripping down his knuckles, knowing there was no undoing this. No victory.

Because the truth was worse than pain.

He had already lost her.

Back in the NICU, Paige and Elliot sat side-by-side under the soft glow of monitors, Charlotte's heartbeat filling the air like music. Its steady rhythm matched something broken inside them both, something that was slowly stitching itself together.

"Just you wait, baby girl," Paige whispered, stroking her daughter's hair. "You and Mummy are going to stay with Grandma for a while. She's going to spoil you rotten."

Chuckling softly, his chest aching with relief, Elliot still had a haunted expression. The unspoken question of what came next.

Paige turned to him, eyes tired but carrying something gentler than before. Hope.

"I think I know what we should call her."

Elliot arched a brow. "She already has a name."

"Yes." Paige's lips curved faintly. "Her name is Charlotte Thea De Luca."

She spoke it like a blessing, each syllable deliberate - a gift wrapped in trust.

Elliot looked at her, mouth agape. The name was not just a name. It was forgiveness. It was belonging. It was the beginning of something he thought he'd lost forever.

"She's yours, Elliot. Ours." Paige's throat tightened, but her voice was steady. "But I need you to understand… I don't choose you; I choose her."

With a groundswell of emotion threatening to bring on more tears, he nodded.

"I know. I do too."

Together they looked down at the small but incredibly perfect girl sleeping on Paige's chest. The outside world still burned with lies and scars, but for the first time it didn't matter. Every wound, every betrayal, every mistake had led them here. To this moment. To her.

To Charlotte.

And in her fragile heartbeat, they found the only kind of forever that mattered.

ONE YEAR LATER

Dear little love,
My Charlotte,

Today you turned one. One whole year of your gorgeous smell, your moods, your fierce determination and laughter. You were made to mend my broken heart, my darling.

Your party was exactly as you would expect it to be, ridiculously chaotic and lots of fun. There were streamers hanging like drunken rainbows, too many cupcakes thanks to your Aunty Grace, a sea of balloons, your Nonna hovered near the cake, crying every fifteen minutes, as she always does when it comes to her Principessa, and you diving head first into icing like a girl starved. Everyone who loves you filled your Grandma Tessie's house with noise and warmth and, for a moment, I just stood still and let it all wash over me. You are so deeply adored, my little love. Not just by me, but by our ever-growing and wonderful village.

While it is your birthday, I feel like I am the one who got the gift – your kidneys are stable. Your latest results came back steady and strong. Unchanged in the best possible way. After a year of appointments, ultra-sounds, surgical consults and holding my breath more times than I'll ever admit, that stability felt like a birthday miracle. A promise that you are moving through this world with a little extra protection.

Then there is your dad.

You might someday hear stories about the year before you were born; stories of heartbreak, distance and bitter-ness running through our lives. But I want you to know this, the moment you crashed into the word he rebuilt himself from the ground up.

He cut out the people who dragged him down. Those who only wished him harm and cast overbearing shadows on his life are gone, and we will never let them dim your light. He stopped the habits that blurred him. He worked slowly and steadily to be the man that you could rely on. He showed up to every appointment, helped with every sleepless night and watched every milestone. No half measures. No disappearing acts. Just a father who would come at the drop of a hat and be there for every bedtime story.

We fought sometimes, healing isn't linear after all, but whenever it came to you we stood as one. Somewhere along the way something softened between us. Not the old love by any means, that will never come back. But something new and steadier. Something hopeful. Something better.

I watched him carry you around today - tired eyes, sticky shirt and the biggest smile I have ever seen. You are the sun our worlds orbit, darling girl.

I don't know what comes next for us. I'm not ready to predict anything beyond what we are now; two people brought together by the power of love and determination to give our daughter everything.

You, my little love, are the best thing to ever happen to us. One day you may read the letters I have written to you. You will read the rawest parts of me and it may change the way you see your dad and I, but I hope that you read it and don't see the flawed individuals we were. I hope you see how love can be transformative; how it can come in so many different shapes and sizes. It can be big and loud like your Poppy Lou's love to tell everyone about you (and show random strangers your pictures) or quiet and subtle like Uncle Jasper's love in the way he calls you Squish.

Here is what I want to leave you with and tuck into your heart as you grow:

You were born in the middle of a storm and somehow became our lighthouse.

You turned the wreckage of our broken hearts into something worth rebuilding.

You taught me how strong I was and that, with your hand in mine, I can put one foot in front of the other.

You changed everything - and I would do it all again

in a heartbeat for you.
  With all my love and adoration,
  Mumma xx

The End

ACKNOWLEDGMENTS

I think the biggest thank you goes to the people who helped me survive this process of bringing *The Lies We Loved* to life.

To Finley, my boy. I poured every fear, every worry and every heartbreaking moment of our journey together through your dialysis into this book. Now, five years on, you've grown into the strongest, funniest, most gloriously imaginative kid - my animal-obsessed, storytelling, Freddie-Mercury-reincarnated legend. Thank you for taking every challenge in your stride and for being exactly who you are.

To Maisie, thank you for the rare, sacred pockets of calm where you slept long enough for me to edit a chapter. For babbling back at me as I talked through ideas, which I obviously took as your enthusiastic approval. You brought light into every exhausted moment.

To Jayke, for fiercely believing in me - even when I didn't. For being the best husband, the best partner and for quietly taking on extra responsibilities when my cup was very, very empty. You held our little world together so I could build this one.

To my mum, Tina, for being the best (and most patient - and free) emotional support human. Thank you for the running commentary as you experienced *The Lies We Loved*. You have always been my biggest cheerleader and my audience for bad jokes.

To my dad, Simon, for bringing the vibes to 3am editing sessions and regularly making me laugh.

To Ashley Horan at Ash Elle Designs, the queen of cover designing! Thank you for being so patient and taking my ridiculous ideas and bringing them to life.

To my beta readers, especially Zahli, thank you for the feedback, the rallying behind me on the late nights I was up editing and talking me off a ledge more times than I can count.

To Ally at The Caffeinated Co for fueling me with caffeine as I sat on the writing stretches and contemplated my life choices.

To everyone else who has been part of this process, no matter how big or small.

Thank you!